Joma West was born in L
later she was moved to Zambia and she hasn't stopped moving ever since. Travelling through Africa, Scotland, China, Italy and Japan, stories were her natural companions. At fifteen, she began making up her own stories to tell her school friends and soon she was writing them all down. She studied English Language and Literature at the University of Glasgow and then took up teaching for a while, because that was a grown-up job.

Joma writes in several genres, but her primary focus is Science Fiction, which she finds exciting, flexible and challenging. Joma likes to use the strange to highlight and interrogate the familiar. Because stories are reflections of ourselves, she believes that, whilst they should definitely entertain, they should also help us understand what it is to be human. She currently lives in between places and supports her writing habit by working part time at the Royal Mail.

WILD

Joma West

First published in Great Britain
Sandstone Press Ltd
7 Dochcarty Road
Dingwall
Ross-shire
IV15 9UG
Scotland

www.sandstonepress.com

The publisher acknowledges support from
Creative Scotland towards publication of this volume.

ISBN: 978-1-910985-30-4
ISBNe: 978-1-910985-31-1

Cover design by Brill
Typesetting by Iolaire Typesetting, Newtonmore
Printed and bound in Great Britain by Clays Ltd, St Ives plc.

Acknowledgements

Writing a book is hard. But writing *Wild* felt easy. A lot of that is because of the people who helped me along the way so this is a small thank you to those who were involved.

Becks Collins handed me the word. I imagine she didn't know where it would lead.

Maya West gave me a home while I wrote.

Ba and Baj watched with endless patience, read without complaining, discussed openly and in depth and edited judiciously.

Peter McCune, my writing companion, tackled every draft, edited, discussed, praised and criticised with supreme generosity. My deadlines were his too and he met them without breaking a sweat.

I would also like to thank the Novella Team for picking this one out of the many, and Lucy English for picking it out of the few. Thanks also to Ciarán Hodgers, for helping with all the practical aspects, and Sandstone Press for delivering a lovely looking object.

Joma West

I swallowed. I was nervous. Everyone at school had been talking about the sims in the word museum for months. It was the new thing, and the longer I stayed away from the museum the less wild I looked to the other kids. And it wasn't like I was popular. That isn't to say I was unpopular. I was just me. I would have liked to not be me but being me was better than being some other people I could think of, so... well what I'm saying is that I wasn't miserable. I was just a kid. Just like all the other kids.

There are things everyone would do to make life better. There are lives everyone wishes they had instead of their own. But in the absence of a fairy godmother I decided to go ahead and do what everyone else was doing. To do the *wild* thing. And I was nervous.

I went on a Saturday morning. I walked there. Our town is small and you can walk pretty much everywhere but most kids ride segs instead of walking. If I'm honest, I'd like to ride a seg too, but my parents can't afford one right now.

Anyway. The museum is in the centre of town. It's up on a hill and in a way it's kind of like a lodestone. It draws the eye. I walked up that hill and stopped to look at the place where I lived: a cheap knockoff town spread out under a dome, the streets and avenues organised in lines and rows in perfect order. Not much of a place. I guess that I felt like I was pretty much the same though, you know? Not much of a person. And this was home.

The word museum had only been open for about an hour, so it was still pretty empty when I walked in.

The last time I had been to the museum I was six and it was a school trip. It wasn't a word museum then, just a regular museum. I'd loved it. My memory of it was so shiny that it seemed weird to me that I was nervous to walk through the doors again. I suppose I didn't really want to lose the museum I still had in my head from all those years ago.

It's an imposing building. I guess most museums are. But when you're six the whole world is enormous, so the museum in my head was practically a planet. The expectations of what I'd find behind those doors were too much for me; I remember bouncing about like a rubber ball. My imagination wasn't big enough for the building and, at that age, my imagination was pretty enormous. I remember it was bright out because the museum was so dark when I stepped inside – so dark I couldn't see anything for a while. It was dark and quiet and cool and I stopped bouncing. It was like walking into a church.

I remember the smell of old things.

The whole day was a wonder. There were so many things to see and, as I walked from room to room, I could feel my world getting bigger and bigger.

I know that the museum in my memory isn't real. If I

walked into *that* museum today I can imagine I would be disappointed. It wouldn't be so big, for a start. The amazing objects would have grown mundane with understanding. Instead of getting larger, I would feel the world shrinking to fit a succession of shabby rooms filled with uninspired scenes that only explained a part of life, the information cards lacking conviction. That's probably what it would be like, but I've been saved that particular brand of disappointment and my romantic ideas can remain intact.

My museum was shut down two years ago. The cost of looking after a bunch of useless objects was too high. Not many people want to look at sarcophagi, vases or animal skeletons anymore, so the people in charge decided it was time to copy the bigger, better museums that lived in bigger, better cities. They dismantled my magical museum, and they turned it into a word museum.

The first ever word museum opened up in Tokyo when I was little. I suppose I was dimly aware of it when it happened but I reckon I had more important things to think about, like my next play-date, or getting the Telekineticopter that was so wild back then. You probably remember it: the helicopter that responds to your thoughts? Anyway, I know more about the Tokyo museum now. People still talk about it because it's meant to be the best in the world. Everyone who can afford to go says how wild it is. I wasn't sure why it was so good until I asked my dad about it. At first he was quiet. You know when you're just about getting old enough to realise that your parents don't actually know everything? Yeah, I reached that point a couple of years ago, but I still like pretending Dad really does know everything. And he still likes pretending it too.

He didn't say anything for a while. And when he did he was kind of just blustering, but one thing he said really struck me. He said that all dictionaries change, depending on the people that compile them, and who they're compiling them for. So a word museum – which is basically a dictionary – is shaped by the people that made it.

If that's the case, it stands to reason that Tokyo might be the best simply because it has the most comprehensive dictionary in the world. So that makes the users' experiences richer and deeper. But the museum in my town is just a poor imitation. All we could afford, all we had access too, limited and limiting. That's a pretty interesting thought. And I wondered, as I walked up to the museum, if it was really worth the effort; if I was just getting a cheap experience, why bother getting any experience at all? It still kind of impressed me, though, and there was one thing I couldn't deny: this was what the wild kids did. And I needed to understand it.

Walking in that second time was strange, because even though I knew it was going to be different from the old museum, I still kind of expected it to be the same. Man, it was *so* different. They had opened up the galleries and the place was incredibly light. White and chrome, screen-friendly lights everywhere, no dark corner to hide treasure in, everything slick, clean, uniform. Row after row of tables, screen after screen of computers, ergonomic chairs all standing in formation, only the ones in use breaking ranks. This museum made a statement. This was the here and now. This was the present, eagerly peeking at the future. The past was history! Who cares! It's gone, over, done! This is a museum not a mausoleum!

As I walked in, a smiling woman approached me.

'Can I help you?' she asked.

I guess maybe she was helpful because it wasn't busy. Maybe she could tell it was my first time there.

'Can I just use any screen?'

'Of course – just pick a free monitor. Have you been to a word museum before?'

I shook my head but, as I did, I knew I should have nodded instead.

'Okay, well let's get you set up at a screen and I can show you how it all works.'

Her smile never wavered. I followed her in. She led me to a monitor and it was one of those moments when you feel like you're being forced into a situation you don't want to be in but social conventions stop you from making your excuses and leaving. First, I didn't really want her help and I was pretty sure I didn't need it. Second, she led me to a monitor I didn't want to be at. It wasn't in one of the spots. You know the places I mean, the spots in a room where you feel most comfortable? This monitor was definitely not in a spot. I didn't like its angle, its proximity to other users, its position in relation to the doorway, or even its position in its own row. It was all wrong. Bad feng shui as my bio teacher, Ms Sneddon, would say. She's kind of weird.

But the lady had led me to this screen, had woken it up, and I knew I would look idiotic if I asked to move now. So I didn't say anything and I wondered if anyone would notice me move places once the woman was gone. I sat down and she leant over my shoulder.

'It's super simple. It explains itself, really,' she said. And it made me wonder: why was she bothering to explain it to me, then? I felt that kind of hot self-conscious feeling you get when you're sure everyone sees you and they're quietly laughing. What if someone I knew saw this woman showing me how to use this machine? It was something everyone else had figured out ages ago.

She pointed to the icons on the screen.

'You can pick out the subject you're interested in. If you move the cursor–' she drifted the cursor over the icons and the movement made me even more aware of her presence as her arm brushed over mine '–over the icon, it tells you which subject each picture represents. If you just want to browse at random hit this icon.' She pointed to a picture of a bizarre-looking animal.

'What is that?' I asked, before I could stop myself and I groaned internally as I said it. She seemed to smile at me again, though I could have sworn she hadn't stopped smiling since I'd met her, so I wasn't sure how that was possible.

'It's a chimera. Those are mythological animals that usually combine elements of several different species of known animal. The original chimera was a combination of a lion, a goat, and a snake, and it could breathe fire. This chimera–' she pointed at the icon again '–was created for this specific museum. See?' I looked at it. 'It's part snake, part elephant, part stag and... crocodile. It has crocodile teeth.' She grinned at me as if she was joking, but she wasn't. I shrugged. What was I supposed to say to that?

'I think I've got it,' I told her, hoping she'd leave then.

'Let me show you a few more things,' she said. 'If you want to search a specific word you click this icon and a search bar will pop up.' She pointed at a book that had the word 'word' on it. 'And I'll just take you through the sims and how they work. Here, let's give the random choices a whirl.'

She clicked on the chimera. The screen went dark for a moment and then seemed to unfold into a photograph. As the photo materialised the woman's smile finally slipped off her face. Not in a sad way or anything, she just finally looked normal is all.

The photograph was a black and white shot of a man holding a saxophone. The word *Jazz* appeared at the top of the screen and I noticed that as the woman moved the cursor over the man in the photo the subheading *John Coltrane* flickered and then faded in and out of sight.

'I'm not sure this is a great one,' the woman said. 'Let's give it another shot,' and she clicked the little chimera again before I could say anything. Not that I really cared what we looked at.

'Oh, this is wild!' she said with a grin, and I looked at the image. It was a cat – black and white, green eyes, lying on its side in the sun. 'You want to try it out?'

I nodded out of habit, though I knew she wasn't really asking.

'Okay, this is how it works. You take the leads and plug them into your wrugs. The leads are sanitised after every user but we keep sanitising gel handy if you want to make sure yourself.' She gestured to a bottle right by the monitor. 'Once you're jacked in and you've pressed play you're immediately immersed in your selected simulation. You ride it out to the end; it's impossible to abort a programme once it's begun, and safety catches click the leads into your wrugs so you can't pull them free by accident or anything. The safety catches disengage at the end of the programme.'

'What prevents me from physically reacting to the sim?' I asked her, kind of relieved that I finally had a real question that justified her presence.

'Your wrugs provide a connection that goes directly to your brain, so everything you perceive within your chosen programme is just code that's been written to stimulate neurons that effect senses. This gives you the sensation of really participating in the programme when actually only your brain is engaged with it. Your body is bypassed altogether. It's pretty remarkable.'

I digested this information. She was making the sim sound really safe but in a way everything she said just frightened me more.

'Thanks,' I said.

'You're welcome.' That smile widened. 'Should we give it a whirl, then?'

I didn't want to try the sim she'd chosen but I felt trapped, so I just nodded like an idiot.

'Okay, plug in!'

I swallowed. Because she was watching, I didn't bother using the sanitising gel, even though I wanted to. I just took the leads and plugged them into my wrugs and I kept telling myself: *Other kids do this all the time. They do it all the time.* I felt even more trapped with my wrists jacked like that. I had never really liked using my wrugs. That thudding buzz as they connected (a bit like an electric shock) made me feel... wrong.

'Are you comfortable?' she asked me.

I nodded again.

'Right. I'll just press play, then. Don't worry,' she said suddenly, putting a hand on my shoulder. 'It's the ride of your life. Enjoy it!'

I guess the whole point of me relaying this is to describe what I experienced so it's kind of ridiculous, me saying how indescribable all of it was. I can't do that. I'll try to be as accurate as possible. Maybe accurate is the wrong word. I'll try to make it as real as I can with just words.

When she pressed play I felt a surge of power flooding through my wrists. And then I didn't have wrists.

The feelings are hard to describe because I didn't experience thoughts like people do. My mind stretched into the body of a cat – sinuous, simple, sun-soaked – and my thoughts weren't really thoughts at all, but impressions of things.

I wonder now if my experience was like everyone else's: a regulated experience designed by the people that programmed our museum. Or did my mind bring something different to the sim? I wondered then, right afterwards, when I was capable of thinking in a way I actually understood: *how did the sim programmers know that this was what it felt like to be a cat? That this was how cats thought*? I did some research later, long after that day in the word museum, and what I understand is this:

Programme coders have access to a huge data bank of animal research, which exists because, once upon a time, people were really interested in understanding animals – how they live, communicate, develop – all that kind of stuff. Apparently they used to experiment on all sorts of creatures, even plants, subjecting them to various stimuli and recording how they responded and what physical reactions were provoked.

What I understand about programming for the word bank is that coders use this research to make neuro-maps. So they used the research on cats to create a neuro-map of all the physical and psychological effects taking place within the animal in response to various stimuli. Then they laid this cat neuro-map over a human one and from there pieced together a picture of how to create a corresponding reaction to specific stimuli in the sim from animal to person.

But this can't be the whole picture. I mean, I'm no scientist, so I figure this is just a layman's way of explaining something beyond me, but I still think there are some holes here. I know very little about animals, but I know that different species had different kinds of brain, and that their brains were designed to support the kind of thinking that was appropriate for their environment. Ms Sneddon once told us that some animals had whole parts of their brains that were entirely absent in our own. If our brains haven't even developed certain parts that some animals had, how could sim coders possibly get any of these animal simulations right? Especially in our little museum, where the coding is probably pretty basic compared with the likes of Tokyo or Jo'burg.

To be fair, I haven't checked to see if they have every animal recorded in the word bank. Perhaps they don't. Maybe some animals remain un-translated. Perhaps cats are one of the few that are easy to transcribe. I'm drifting away from the story again. Sorry.

You're probably wondering what it felt like to be a cat? It felt warm. That's the first word that comes to mind. I felt overwhelmingly warm. I wasn't just warm from the sun, or the air circulating between the fine hairs on my body, or from the warmth of the stone slab I was stretched out on. I was warm inside – my organs, my thoughts; I vibrated with it and those vibrations buzzled up my throat like soda and spread out of my mouth as noise. I stretched. My body felt so long, so soft and relaxed and yet I also felt that I was coiled up around a spring of tension. I was gazing out through sleepy eyes, half shut and the world appeared enormous. But I didn't feel small. I didn't feel large. I just felt present in a way I never had before. As if I was attached to everything I saw, a part of it all. And yet apart and free and unfettered. None of these words quite fit. It's like I'm trying to make the jigsaw of the image on the box only all the pieces in the box actually belong to different jigsaws.

I felt alive.

Not that I don't feel alive normally. I guess what I'm trying to say is that my attention was focussed on my livingness. My state of being alive. I don't think I usually pay much attention to that. I reckon most people's attention is so diverted that they forget the fact that they're alive. It isn't something to sit around thinking about, really. There are too many things to do. But not if you're a cat lounging in the sun. Again, I want to clarify things but I'm not quite sure how to. It's not like, as a cat, I was sitting there thinking about my aliveness. I don't know if I was thinking at all. I couldn't even say, after being a cat, if cats actively think about anything. It was just something I was aware of. One thing I was aware of out of many many things.

The feeling of aliveness, livingness, of being alive – it was intoxicating. But not like being drunk. I've been drunk once. I was at a party and my friend, Kel, convinced me it would be wild to have some drinks. She wasn't wrong. It was fun, and I felt alive then too but everything was soft and unclear. Whereas being the cat was piercingly clear. I was seeing things in a way I'd never seen them before; everything was familiar, but the whole world had become new. I get it now, why the woman liked this sim. Why she suggested I try it. I get why everyone talks about the sims, goes into them, loves them. I get it.

BUT....

After describing all this aliveness you may think I'm not being honest when I write this next thing:

I thought it was sick.

See, I felt all these things, and when I read what I've written now it sounds like a magical experience. But for me it wasn't, because *I* wasn't there. It wasn't me in a cat. Though I guess part of me must have been there in order for me to remember it all. I just recall that there was no *me*. I lost myself. I felt a strange sense of vertigo in my displacement. No, it was stronger than vertigo, but I don't have a word for it. I need to look for one, but I can't stop just yet. If I find the word I'll put it down but for now I just want to press on.

I rode that sim out – it wasn't long – and when it ended I snapped into myself with a force that stung. My wrists hummed as the locks in the leads disengaged and if I hadn't been so disorientated right then I think I would have ripped the things out of my wrugs immediately. But I was confused. I'd been displaced and re-placed in what felt like just a moment.

Eventually, I had enough presence of mind to unplug. And after that I think I just sat and stared at the computer screen for a while. I didn't think about it then, but I guess the woman had left after I started riding.

I went into the word museum that day with a mission in mind. Being a cat for ten minutes was not part of that mission but the experience was disturbing enough to make me think about getting up and leaving without doing what I had come to do. I'm pretty stubborn, though (I get it from my mother), so I decided to stay.

And I typed in the word I had gone there to find and understand. *Wild*.

Before I go into it, let me tell you why.

Everything good is *wild*. It's the word we use when something's worth something. Sims are wild, hacking is wild, scary things are wild. Wild is what you want to be, wild is how you want to look, wild is what you want to have. Who would touch you if you didn't have any wildness? What are you if you aren't wild? What does it mean if the things you like, the people you like, the world you want to inhabit isn't wild? What does it say about you? More importantly, what does it say about *me*? I'm not one of the wild kids. I'm not tame either (*I'm not*), so where do I stand? And how do I decide where I draw the line? What do *I* want? How can I choose if I don't really know what wild means? Some kids just know it. They couldn't tell you if you asked them, but they know it like they know to breathe in and out. You can tell those kids from the other ones, the ones that try. I don't ever want to be one of the ones that try. I just want to understand.

Wild *a.*, *adv.*, *& n.* 1. *A.* (Of animal or plant) not domesticated or cultivated (esp. of species or varieties allied to others that are not wild; *wild beast, plant; wild ass, duck, rose, vine)*; not civilised, barbarous; (of scenery etc.) having conspicuously desolate appearance; **~ and woolly,** lacking refinement(s), barbarous. **2.** (Of horse, game-bird, etc.) shy, given to shying, easily startled, hard to get near. **3.** Unrestrained, wayward, disorderly, irregular, out of control, unconventional, (*a wild fellow; settled down after a wild youth; hair hanging in wild locks; living in wild times; room is in a wild disorder*); (of playing-card) having any rank chosen by player holding it.; **run ~**, grow or stray unchecked or undisciplined or untrained. **4.** tempestuous, violent, (*a wild wind, night*). **5.** intensely eager, excited, frantic, passionate, distracted, mad, (*is wild with excitement, to try it; wild delight, excitement, enthusiasm, grief, rage*); (of looks, appearance, etc)indicating distraction; (colloq.) angry, infuriated; **~ about**, enthusiastically devoted to (person or subject); **drive ~**, madden. **6.** haphazard, rash, ill-considered, ill-aimed, disturbed by excitement, (*a wild guess, shot, blow, venture; wild opinions, bowling*). **7. ~ boar,** tusked wild pig (*Sus scrofa*) from which domesticated pigs are descended; **~ cat,** medium-sized wild feline, esp. European species (*Felis sylvestris*); **~ ' cat** (fig.) hot-tempered or violent person; ~ ' cat *a.*, reckless, financially unsound, (of strike) sudden and UNOFFICIAL, (of well) drilled for oil etc. where there is only a possibility of success; **~ ' fire,** = *Greek* FIRE1, will-o'-the-wisp, (fig.) thing that spreads rapidly; **~ ' fowl,** game-bird(s); **~ - goo'se chase,** foolish or hopeless or fruitless quest; **~ horse,** horse not domesticated or broken in (*'horses would not drag* etc. *it from me,* I refuse to disclose the secret); *wild* HYACINTH ; **~ ' life,** wild animals collectively; **~ man,** (1) savage (2) political extremist; ~ *man of the woods,* orang-utan; *wild* OATS ; **~ rice,** tall grass of genus *Zizania* yielding edible grains; **~ silk,** silk from wild silkworms, or imitation of this from short silk fibres; *wild* THYME ; **W ~ West,** western US in time of lawlessness; **~ ' wood,** (poet.) uncultivated or unfrequented woodland. **8.** Hence ~ ' ISH1 *2 a.*, ~ ' LY2 *adv.*, ~ ' NESS *n.* **9.** *adv.* In wild manner (*shooting wild*). **10.** *n.* desert, wild tract; **(out) in the ~ s,** (colloq.) far from towns etc. [OE *wilde* = OS, OHG *wildi*, ON *villr*, Goth. *wiltheis*, f. Gmc * *wilthijaz*]

Wild – that's it. That's what it means. I can read and I understand. Is that enough? Do I have to go into it?

I need to remind you that I'm using words to describe this, but words mean nothing. They don't get close to the experience. I'm applying human translation to something beyond human.

Looking back now, I'm in two minds about what I did. I think, overall, I'm glad I went through with it. But man,

I... no. I won't start telling you things like that. It's best just to try and show it all, from start to finish. I just want you to know that this changed me. I went in as me and I came out totally different. I don't care so much anymore. About this, about the other kids, about being wild. And looking back at it all now, I know I'm interpreting it through different eyes than the eyes that saw it all. So what you're getting, isn't exactly what I felt. Not that it ever could be. Okay. Here we go.

I picked up the leads – what was the point of sanitising them now? – and I plugged them back into my wrugs. Thud, buzz, hum, zwoosh... jacked in. Trapped. No, I wasn't trapped yet. But then I pressed play.

Zwoom!

1

A. (Of animal or plant) not domesticated or cultivated (esp. of species or varieties allied to others that are not wild; *wild beast, plant; wild ass, duck, rose, vine)*; not civilised, barbarous; (of scenery etc.) having conspicuously desolate appearance; ~ **and woolly,** lacking refinement(s), barbarous.

I breathe in deep and then blow out, my thick lips rippling against each other, rumbling a whicker. My barrel belly narrows then swells with my next inhalation. I am sniffing the evening, picking up cooling earth, the musk of a passing goat, dry dung that marks the territory. And I am listening.

Listen. A bird skrees a mile away; a warning cry, but not for me. The hoof falls of the goat recede as it meanders away. Sand and rock tumble; the rock skitters, clicking, clacking, grating, but the sand only hisses. A slither – what does a slither sound like? Shifting sand, a slight crunch and a hiss, not coming this way. Listen. A distant snort. I know that voice. She whickers to her young. Listen. The wind rises, a tree creaks, old, familiar, soothing. Listen. A hoof fall, a sigh, a soft snort – who's this?

Sniff. Who's this? Too far away, too far. Sand and rock shift beneath my hooves as I pick a path down the hill, move in from my border, follow my ears, negotiate the land in the growing darkness, not difficult, sure hooves, I know this country, my land, my territory, my dung marks it, it's mine, but who's this? Who's this? Sniff. Listen. Sniff. Listen. I don't recognise that voice. Sniff. Musk. Male. Intruder. How close is he? How close to my herd? Listen. Familiar voice, she whickers to her young. Listen. Unfamiliar voice, he snorts, he snorts, is he snorting at her? Listen. Cry:

'HEEEEEEEAwwwww!'

Good. That carried. Listen.

'HEEEAwww!' She cries. Good girl. Move. Listen. Where is he? He's moving. Listen. Hooves thud on sand and click against rock. He hears me. He's standing firm! Where is he? Sniff, listen. Dark ahead but I can see him. He's standing square. He's waiting! Ears back. Show him. My territory.

Square up. Stop. Toss my head. My territory. Mine. Understand. You can be here. Yes. You can be here. By. My. Leave. No. Stay away from her. Stay away from my herd. My territory. My herd. By. My. Leave. Understand?

Listen. I see. Invasion. I see. Square up!

I move fast. I stand up high, I rear, I kick quick hooves. He is young, younger than me, not so big, not so strong, not so clever, not so much. He rears up and hooves clash – lash out, lash out! Come down and spin, quick I am, I am so quick! Spin around and kick and kick. Listen.

Hooves thud. His belly sounds hollow, kick, and kick, try to bite, tear his skin, teach him a lesson, invader. And the skin tears, it does, he is young, he squeals, he squeals, he squeals,

I squeal,

I scream–

'–WAAAAAACKWACKWACK' I scream! I soar! The sky, the sky! Where are the others? Formation. Let's get into formation.

'WAAAAAAACKWACKWACKWACK!'

But now isn't the time. No. Fly, fly, fly, find water, down, down, down, my feet they slide into the lake, so soft, warm weightlessness, my body settles, water creeps through my feathers and cups my bottom. I float. And then kick, kick, kick off I go, GULP! DUCK! Down I go, dark down here, snap! Caddisfly! Snap! Snap! Snap! Shake my head and kick on. On I go. Alone. Where are the others? Nesting. Yes, nesting.

'WAAAACKWACKWACKWACKWACKWACKWA CKWACK!' Who's that?

Plop. Plop. Plop. Plop. Four bodies land. Oh. I can feel the hunger. Nesting time. Nesting. They haven't found one. Oh no. No. Kick, kick, kick, move on, swim on, go on, get away.

'Waaaaaaackwackwackwackwack,' says one.

'Waaaackwackwack,' says another.

Kick on, they kick on, they swim after me. I must go, kick on kick on kick on and harder, don't let them come on, don't let them gain, swim. Swim swim swim swim SWIM!

Nesting time, they must have a mate, they have no mate and I am alone. Swim on! They come on after me. They chase; four of them, four drakes, they chase and me I'm chased, I'm chaste. My heart beats harder and I must fly, I must go on, I swim, I swim, they swim, they swim, four of them and me. I swim and then–

'WAAAAAACKWACKWACKWACKWACK!' I scream! I soar! The sky, the sky; there's more space here to fly, to fly. And on they come, they fly, they fly, four of them and I. My heart beats harder, my wings beat harder, I fly I fly I fly, but on they come they come they come, on they come they come. They come on. Bigger than me, and on they come and I feel the air as their wings beat and they come on to me and down they come and –

'WAAAAAAACK!' It hurts. He pecks, he pecks, it hurts. 'WAAAAAACKWACK!' It hurts. Two peck at me, they peck, they peck, it hurts. 'WAAAAAACKWACKWACK!' They jostle me, chase me, come on to me, force me lower, I fly lower, I am lower and lower, I twist, I try to fly, my heart beats harder, my wings beat harder, I turn, but they are bigger, stronger, faster, and they come on. They force me down. They peck at me, they peck and peck and peck and peck 'WAAAACKWACKWACK!' it hurts! My heart beats harder and I run on and they come on and I feel so very tired! I can't get away. On they come, they come, they come, on they come, they come on! I can't run, I want to run, I can't run, I want to fly, to scream! To soar! To fly! I can't fly on, I can't swim on, I can't run on, I can't go on and, on they go. They go on, and I crawl. I crawl.

I climb.

I wind.

Rosa. Rosa Canina. I get my hooks into you. Pierce, claw and crawl up. You don't see me grow but you see me grown. You want me? Come here creature, but be careful. I could get my hooks into you. Careful. Settle.

Come inside – what have you got for me? Pollinate me, yes, yes come inside. Careful as you leave. I could get my hooks into you. Yes, I could get my hooks into you.

I can't get out. I'm locked in. I have to ride this out to the end.

I became myself suddenly. I could still feel some alien excitement in my guts, a strange sexuality I wanted to forget but it was making my body hum in a not unpleasant way. I looked down thinking: *I have to get out of here, I have to unplug*. But I wasn't plugged in. The confusion didn't last too long. I looked for the computer screen to find I was nowhere I had ever seen before. I wasn't out yet. I remember wondering: *now that I'm myself what the hell else is going to happen?*

I looked first. That's something I realised afterwards, when I returned to my life: I always use my eyes first. I was standing in a landscape that stretched out, empty, all the way to where the sky meets the earth. The ground under my feet was cracked. Dry clay. There were rocks. Not many, just some here and there, breaking up the flatness.

I stood there, looking at the emptiness for... I don't know how long. It felt like it could have been years. Emptiness. No city. No people. *Real* sky (I've never seen real sky. I reckon you haven't either). And nothing. I stood there, waiting for what might come next. But nothing happened. So I took a step, leaving a pair of footprints in the clay behind me, and beneath me more clay cracked. I bent down and touched it. It was smooth and warm. I rubbed my fingers over it and then looked at my hands. They were covered in a fine red dust. I sniffed them. They smelled like baked earth. A kind of old smell, dirty, but the clean sort of dirt, the kind that doesn't hurt you, the kind we don't get much of. I felt along the cracks and broke off a jagged piece of clay. I was surprised by how light it felt, how flat and smooth it was. A piece of dirt I wasn't supposed to play with, that looked just like a broken fragment of that crockery set my mother loves; antiques she rescued, pieces of the old world when outside really was *outside*. I pressed the clay between my fingers and was surprised by how easily it crumbled. Now you see it, now you don't.

Finally, I stood up and walked. It was all I could think to do. I walked and I tried to make sense of what had gone just before. I tried to put words to the indescribable. Words I just wrote, words you just read and understood, about something you will never understand. Unless you go there yourself.

But it was more than just putting words to it. I was trying to come to terms with the feelings I had when I finally understood what had happened. The beginning wasn't hard for me. The sensation of being able to hear like that, to know everything that was happening in the darkness of my domain... and transforming, flying! It was thrilling. It was unbelievable. It was wild. And then my heart beat harder. The empty space around me reeled as I felt so small in my body again. And it hurt! I could feel the weight of a drake on my back and the hardness of his beak as he bit my neck. I could feel the...

I don't want to talk about this. Maybe I shouldn't have started.

Look. I want to be honest. I mean, there's a point to me telling everything but some of this... maybe I can just put the experiences into words. You know – describe the indescribable. But I don't think I can tell everything. About how I felt.

As I walked through the emptiness, I had to go through it all again, this time as myself with my thoughts and my feelings and my reactions. It made me sick, thinking about it. I had to keep walking. That was all I could do.

When I had finally thought through it all, remembered enough, felt sick enough, endured enough, I started to think about the nothing around me. Feeling it with all my senses. Not just seeing the emptiness, the red ground, the blue sky, or even the baked dirt smell, but feeling the heat. The sun was at my back, sinking in through my shirt. I was sweating, dark patches spreading under my arms, and beads rolling down my face leaving salt tracks on my skin.

The heat began to sap my energy. I thought maybe I could stop and rest. If only there was some shade, maybe I could stop and rest. But there was nothing. *If I stopped now*... there was nothing and no one. What would I do? I was alone and there was nothing I could do. I didn't know how I got to this place. *Where did I arrive? I must have come from somewhere, I must be going somewhere. Why did I come here? Who left me here? Where did I come from?*

I started to run, weak and thirsty but panic driving me on. There had to be an end to the emptiness. *It can't go on forever. Can it? I have to have come from somewhere. Right?* But when I thought about it I couldn't remember where I was before. I couldn't remember the faces of anyone I'd met. *Were there other people? Or am I making them up? Wait... I'm a person. There has to be other people. Or... what am I? What is this place? Why am I running?* I slowed to a walk. *What am I looking for? What... why do I care? What...? Oh.*

I stopped.

This is nowhere. I am nothing. Nothing is happening. Nothing ever was.

2

(Of horse, game-bird, etc.) shy, given to shying, easily startled, hard to get near.

What is that? Up there? A shape? Only I don't know what 'that' or 'up' or 'shape' is. I don't know what a word is, or a thing. How can I tell you what it's like to lose yourself after you've found yourself again? There's a shape on the horizon, and there's me, not sure about who or what I am, unaware that there has ever been anything other than the desolation I'm standing in. And with my empty headedness comes a total acceptance of everything. I saw a shape on the horizon and I don't recall questioning it much. I just watched it coming closer, getting bigger, and as it approached words slotted themselves into places in my head and thoughts began to form. It wasn't just a shape. It was an animal. A horse. It wasn't just coming closer. It was running. Do they run? Horses? No, it's some fancy word – galloping. It was galloping towards me.

I could hear its hooves thudding against the clay – doodoodoodoof, doodoodoodoof, doodoodoodoof, doodoodoodoof – and I think I started nodding my head to the rhythm.

The hooves beat. My heart beat. My wings beat. No. I didn't have wings. I watched the horse come closer. Doodoodoodoof. The rhythm was mesmerising. I'd never seen anything so beautiful. But then I had never seen anything at all. I was new to my thoughts. This something, this creature, this horse was the most beautiful thing I'd ever seen. When I think about it now it still is the most beautiful thing I've ever seen. I'll never see anything with such new eyes again.

The horse galloped. I watched the muscles rippling under its skin. Its legs, mane, tail were black, but the rest of its body was gold. And though words were coming to me – understanding was there – I didn't think anything of the fact that this beautiful, fast creature was heading right towards me. I didn't move. I just existed there, an idiot in the middle of nowhere, watching.

It rushed at me. It didn't even notice my presence. Until the last moment. Doodoodoodoof, doodoodoodoof, doodoodoodoof, doodoodoodoof, my self-preservation kicked in. Doodoodoodoof, doodoodoodoof, doodoodoodoof, doodoodoodoof, I moved, it shied, jumping to the side; it squealed and I moved away, but not fast enough. It squealed and kicked out in panic. I felt the air rush by my face as a hoof missed my cheek. It reared up, afraid, waving its forelegs high above me. It reared over me and as it came down I knew it was going to hit me. The hooves descended doodoof. Thud.

'Eeehuuuuuuh!' I gulped in air by the gallon as I sat up, looking around wildly, trying to locate the horse, trying to find an escape route, I needed to get away. But there was no horse.

'Ssh!' a voice hissed and I turned to look.

A man was crouched down in the grass behind me. Grass!

'Where am I?'

'Shut up!' the man whispered.

I wasn't unplugged, I wasn't out yet, there was more to come. So I got to my knees and watched.

The man crept forwards until he was next to me. He was holding a rifle. I'd never seen a rifle in real life before but I knew what it was. I'd seen one like this, in the old museum, and I'd seen them in classic vids. And of course there were the little wooden pistols my mum gave me.

The man glared at me before creeping ahead. In his wake, crawling on its belly, was one of the most vicious looking dogs I had ever seen. Not that I'd ever seen a real dog. I heard people used to keep them as pets so I guessed this one was a pet. I was back in time somehow. I didn't quite get it but I figured I was about to get another dose of wildness.

The dog didn't deign to notice me, just crawled on after the man. I started to follow but the man turned back and gave me a warning look that froze me where I was. So I just watched them as they crept on. Then he stopped. He muttered something and the dog started to run. It was still crouched low but now it was running ahead and:

'PEHKUUUUUUUUUUUUUUUUK!'

A bird exploded into the air making me jump. My heart was beating hard from the fright but my eyes were up, watching it fly and I started to laugh at myself for being scared of nothing.

'BANG!'

I jumped again. My eyes closed for just a moment. When I opened them again I couldn't see the bird. I heard the dog bark and the man shout out and I knew that the bird wasn't flying anymore.

'Did you see that?' The man called back to me. 'That's how it's done.'

I looked at him. He was smiling. It made me shiver. I blinked and looked up at the empty sky. I think I was still sort of hoping to see the bird again. I laughed at myself but this time I was scared of something.

3

Unrestrained, wayward, disorderly, irregular, out of control, unconventional, (*a wild fellow; settled down after a wild youth; hair hanging in wild locks; living in wild times; room is in a wild disorder*); (of playing-card) having any rank chosen by player holding it. ; **run ~**, grow or stray unchecked or undisciplined or untrained.

I looked up at the sky. It was blue, but as I looked it grew darker. And lighter. And whiter. And it wasn't a sky at all, but a ceiling. And when I looked down I was standing in a room. A maddening, strange room. I assumed there were many tables (though I couldn't see one) from the unnatural height of some of the piles of books. Real books, the old kind made with paper. I saw strange objects poking out of a recess in the wall, and an arm that made me jump until I realised it belonged to a mannequin. I guessed the recess was a fireplace. I had seen pictures of fireplaces. There were shelves coming out at all heights on the walls, some of them so slanted they had no function. I could see the edge of a bed in one corner, but couldn't see the bed itself, covered as it was in clothes and papers, magazines, books, plates, cups, even a trophy and… I knew there was a floor because I could feel it beneath my feet but I couldn't see it. A light was hanging down from the ceiling and it was on. I couldn't see a window anywhere.

I could just make out the door at the other end of the room. As I spotted it, it opened and a man walked in. The man was the room personified. He wore an assortment of clothes, layered up thick, and it was only when I noticed *them* that I realised how cold the place was. His face was difficult to make out: he had a large beard obscuring half of his features, and long matted hair, obscuring the other half. In the dim light I fancied I saw his eyes glitter through his tangled fringe. I couldn't tell if he was surprised to see me in his room or not, but he didn't say anything, so I guessed he wasn't. He seemed only to glance at me before he picked his way over the junk that covered the ground. Then he hurled himself forwards, at a pile of stuff, and landed relatively softly, on what seemed to be an armchair. A crunching sound gave the impression of something breaking underneath him and I hoped it was something inanimate.

He looked at me again.

'So. Should we have at it?'

'Have at what?'

'The game! The game? Why else are you here, you prat? As if I would invite you in? Fuck off! Fuck off!'

There was something in his tone that made me feel he really meant that. And there was something about both him and his room that made me feel I really wanted to do just that. I took a step towards the door and he immediately started again:

'Come on, old friend! Don't be like that! We have a game to play, don't leave me like this.'

I looked back at him and he grinned at me, his teeth bared between all the hair on his face, and I really didn't want to stay. I took another step away.

'Look! Please don't do this; I need the money. Just play one game with me. Just one! I promise I won't go off, I–'

'–You need the money? You think you've already won, do you?'

I didn't know where the words had come from, but they came out of my mouth. The man grinned at me again.

'Take a seat.'

'Oh, can't you be civilised for once in your life, Brendan? We can't play on a pile of shit. At least clear a fucking table.'

Again, the words just came out of me. And it wasn't just that they weren't my words (I don't like to swear), my voice was different too. I sounded older. And old-fashioned. And meaner. I sounded like someone else. But I was still in there, watching it all.

The man stood up and looked for a table. When he found one he swept an arm across it, throwing everything on it onto the floor. I winced at the crash and looked at the mess in dismay. It was disgusting. He gave a pair of chairs the same treatment and then perched them unevenly on the crap on the floor, at either end of the table. He gestured to the table and chairs and bowed. I felt a tight smile cross my face and I picked my way over to a chair. I watched him feel around in his pockets until he found a deck of cards. He put them on the table before sitting down. I looked at my own seat. It was filthy; years of dust, dirt, spilled food and drink, mildew and mould were competing to occupy the space. I thought I saw something crawl over it and when I looked closer I realised it reminded me of a picture I'd seen once: a small thing called a woodlouse. There wasn't just one, though: there were masses, grey lumps rippling down the chair back and looking for somewhere dark. I gritted my teeth and sat down, thinking *it washes off, it all washes off.*

He cut the cards and shuffled. I watched his hands flip, split and riffle them into randomness. Then he dealt. The game began. He went first. He put down his card and I put mine on top. We continued, picking up speed as we went, our eyes trained on the numbers as we ran through the deck until...

'SNAP!' He cried out.

I couldn't argue. He took his cards and we began again.

'SNAP!' My turn.

'SNAP!' Him.

'SNAP!' Him.

'SNAP!' Me.

'SNAP!' Him. Hang on.

'Hang on, you bastard. That isn't a pair.'

'Sure it is. Eights are wild.'

'Since when?'

'We've always played eights wild.'

'No, we haven't.'

'Yes, we have. Let go of my hand.'

I saw I had grabbed his hand as he had moved to pull his cards to him. I thought about it.

'No. You're cheating.'

'Cheating! Am I, fuck! I never cheated in my life. You want to talk cheating let's look at you, you little shit.'

'We've never played eights wild,' I said and I could hear my voice getting harder and colder.

'You bitch!' he spat at me. 'We've never not played them wild!'

I looked at him and wasn't sure how far I wanted to push this. But the other me, the one that kept speaking like I was old and knew this person and had been playing this game over and over and over again, was sure I did want to keep pushing this.

My grip on his hand tightened and I looked him hard in the face, as if my eyes could strike.

'We've never played wilds. Ever. Nice try. Now give up the cards and I'll pretend this never happened.'

He laughed at me then. It was a slow chuckle at first but it gathered into one of those laughs you know isn't going to end any time soon. I don't think it was one of those laughs that would usually upset me, but I could feel this anger growing; a hot anger I'd never felt before. The centre of me clenched up with tension and I felt like it was all I could do not to move from where I was sitting. Then, before I even registered my intent, I reached across the table and slapped him hard across the face; the snap of our skin connecting sounded loud in my ears.

I pulled my hand back in a rush and looked at him nervously. At least I was nervous; the other me wasn't. He rubbed a hairy cheek and looked at me.

'I forgot you had a sting.' He broke into a smile. 'It was worth a try!' He let go of the cards. 'Should we carry on?'

I nodded and took a hold of my pile of cards, knocking them gently into order and pinching the top card, ready to flip it. I watched him do the same. And then he exploded out of his chair. He leapt across the table and grabbed my head between his hands, pulling it forward and smashing it into the wooden surface below us. I don't think I felt that first blow, but I felt my neck straining as he yanked my head up again. Then I felt the blinding pain as he cracked my head against the table a second time, the skin on my forehead splitting open on impact, and up my head was pulled, ready to crash once more. And again and again and again. My thoughts became incoherent. All I noticed was how much it hurt. And the strength of him; I don't think it even occurred to me to fight. I just let him pummel the table with my face. I was dimly aware of the bones in my nose crunching together as it was crushed into the tabletop. I felt my lip split and I could taste blood. Then it was dark and I was gone.

When I opened my eyes I was looking up at grey sky. I'd barely registered the change when I heard a giggle and I turned to find a girl pressed up close to me. She had dark skin – smooth and shining like onyx. Her eyes were warm and they had a wicked glint. She looked at me and laughed properly then. I sat up and I remember the girl sort of vanished from my perception; I was too preoccupied with my surroundings. We were lying on some grass in a park.

I remember now, thinking then, that I had been so much closer to nature in this sim world than I had ever been in the real one. I'd never lain on grass in my life. It wasn't as soft as I had imagined and it prickled through my clothes, but it smelled amazing. Then the girl pinched me, which made me jump.

'What're you lookin' at?' she asked, pressing her face close to mine. The proximity unsettled me. I shifted backwards, but she shifted with me.

'Nothing.'

'Here,' she said and she held out a hand. I looked at it. In the middle of her palm was something red, wrapped in plastic. It looked like a throat lozenge or something, but I wasn't sure because I wasn't allowed to have those at home.

'What is it?' I asked her.

She gave me a funny look.

'Are you crazy? It's a top up. You're coming down. Keep up!' and she unwrapped the red thing and pressed it to my lips, forced it between them, and I didn't have a choice but to open up and swallow. As the red thing went into my mouth and down my throat. I felt as though I had gone into my mouth and down my throat too, and the world transformed. The air became solid – contracting, squeezing me to someplace else. It felt hot and wet and red and I was being squeeeeeeeezed. I started to panic, sliding forwards, I struggled against it and then I felt a hand on my hand. I felt it grasp me. And the girl spoke:

'Keep up!' Her voice sounded so easy and I couldn't help but relax and as I did: Whhhhoooooooooossssssssssshh-hhhhhhh!

We came out of the throat of the world to emerge on the grass where I found her and there she still was, holding my hand and laughing, pulling me to my feet, running, dragging me behind her. I ran like I hadn't run before, caught up in how interesting it felt, how fast, difficult, painful. She called out:

'Keep up!'

She was running so fast. I was breathing heavy and my legs felt leaden, the inside of my throat was raw, but she was just running on and on and I didn't think she would stop. And she was still laughing!

When she did stop and turn to me, it was so sudden I crashed into her and she bounced backwards, laughing even more. Then she grabbed my hands and began spinning. She spun me round and round and round until I thought I might be sick with the dizziness of it.

'Are you flying yet?' she asked.

I shook my head and half sat half fell to the ground.

'No, I think I'm sailing. I feel seasick.' But I didn't know what that felt like! We all knew there used to be seas but...

She laughed again.

'Come on! Keep up!' She pulled me to my feet and led me to a doorway. And then we were on steps and she was running up and calling to me to keep up, keep up! her voice echoing against the hard stone of the well we climbed. I ran as hard as I could, not daring to drop back, too afraid to be on my own, but she was ahead and the distance kept growing.

'Keep up!' she called and I kept running.

I reached the top and burst out onto the roof of a tall building. I looked around for the girl and saw her standing on a wall.

'Are you flying yet?' she asked me. She laughed and tossed her head.

'What are you doing?'

'Keep up,' she smiled at me, and she stepped off the building and vanished.

I screamed and ran to the edge. Perhaps I thought I could reach her even though she was gone. I threw myself against the wall and looked over, half fearing, half hoping to see her body. And I did. She was lying on the roof of a smaller building, about five feet down, rolling around and laughing raucously. I hissed, irritated I'd been fooled, and yet relieved I'd only been fooled. I sat on the wall, swung my legs over, and jumped down. I lay beside her and began to laugh too. We laughed for as long as we could, our sides aching, our faces sore, our throats dry.

'Are you flying yet?' She asked me.

'No,' I said.

'Come on,' and she drew me up and down another set of stairs and we were running outside again and she was taking me somewhere else to do something else, and I was following a whirling mass of energy: the girl who couldn't stop, and all she said was 'Keep up! Keep up!'

Finally, she slowed to a walk. She smiled and asked:

'Do you want to fly?'

'Yes.'

'Keep up!' She stepped onto a metal pipe and walked carefully along it. I followed her. 'Keep your balance!' We walked, concentrating hard, but our balance got harder to keep as we went. I wasn't sure why at first. It finally dawned on me that the ground was shaking. Startled by this, losing concentration, I slipped off the pipe and onto the ground beside it. I looked up at her and saw her flicker in the lights. The train was coming. She was walking on the line, heading for it. She was playing that game. Chicken. I never understood why it was called that. What's a chicken got to do with anything? This was just a game of crazy.

'Get out of the way!' I shouted.

She laughed.

'Get out of the way!' I shouted again.

She laughed harder. She was laughing so hard she couldn't walk anymore but she never stepped off the line. She stood there, doubled over with laughter. And the train was coming.

'GET OUT OF THE WAY!' I screamed.

The train was coming, the train was coming, the train was coming, lights shining bright, throwing her body into silhouette, the sound of the engines drowning out my screams and her laughter, and I could feel the engine in my chest, running faster than my thoughts, an engine going straight through my head and it was coming it was coming it was coming it came it went and I was left there, eyes blinded by the whiteness of the lights, the engine still pounding in my chest. I looked wildly for her, but I couldn't see, and all I could hear was the chook, chook, chook of the train, and then, suddenly... she was still laughing! I don't think I'd ever felt so angry before. She had jumped off the line just in time, jumped to the other side so I never saw her, and the train had distracted me too much to notice, the fear had kept me from seeing, and I was suddenly so angry I wanted to punch her in the face.

I left her laughing behind me, followed the train back the way I'd come. I think she ran on; someone who just kept running, nothing to hold her back. She was running, running, running. No one could keep up.

4

tempestuous, violent, (*a wild wind, night*).

Dark. Dark still silent. Tshooo, ripple nudges soft tshoooooo tshoooooo tshoooooo ripple nudges pushes; pushes nudges soft soft… nudges pushes, pushes, pushes, whoooooooooooooooooooooooooooooooooo! Whoo ooooooooooooooooooooooooooooooo!

Yeeeeah! Whoooooooooooooooooooooooooooo oooo! PUSHES! PUSHES! PUSHES!

WHOOOOOOOO HOOOOOOWWWWWWWL WHOOOOOOOOO! Harder pushes harder! Ripple ridge ride rode road pushes past. Pushes past through over under around in pushes in through pushes through pushes through pushes thrrrroooooooooouuuuggggggh! Whooooooooooo! Hoooooooooowwwwwwwwooooooooo oooooooooooooooooooooooooooo!

HOOOOOOOOWWWWWOOOOOOOOOOO OOOOOOOOOOOOOOOOO!

HOOOOOOOOWWWWWWOOOOOOOOOOO
OOOOOOOOOOOOOOOOOO!

HOOOOOOOOWWWWWWOOOOOOOOOOO
OOOOOOOOOOOOOOOOOO!

PUSH!

Hoooooooooooowwwwwwwwwoooooooooooooooooo
ooooooooooooooooooooooooo!

Push. Push.

Whooooooooooooooooooooooooooooooooooooooo
oooooooooooooooooooooooooo!

Push.

Tshooooooooooooooooooooooooooooooooooooooo
oooooooooooooooooooooooooo!

Nudge.

Ripple.

Ripple nudges soft. Tshoooooo Tshoooooo Tshoooooo

Silent still dark. Dark.

5

> intensely eager, excited, frantic, passionate, distracted, mad, (*is wild with excitement, to try it; wild delight, excitement, enthusiasm, grief, rage*); (of looks, appearance, etc) indicating distraction; (colloq.) angry, infuriated; ~ **about**, enthusiastically devoted to (person or subject); **drive ~**, madden.

'Are we nearly there yet? Are we nearly there yet? Are we nearly there yet?' me.

'If you don't quieten down, I'm going to turn this car around and take us home!'

'Shhhhh!' (to myself.) 'But,' (in a whisper) 'how long will it take to get there?'

Laughter.

'About thirty minutes left, hun. Just bottle some of that excitement for when we get there!'

Bouncing on the car seat, looking at the world flash by. Zoom! Zoom! Zoom! Car, trees, car, car, car, house. Each zoom is a second closer. Bounce bounce bounce!

The car stops. Quick, open the door, little feet pelt the tarmac, run forwards!

'Come back here and take your bag!'

Race around, about turn and run back at Mum. Grab the bag, got my things, keep running, run to the gateway, water park! We made it. We're at the water park! Next stop, Master Blaster Water Winder!

'Let me in, let me in, let me in!'

Laughter.

'Let's just wait a minute for your mum, why don't we?'

'Why? I have my things!'

Laughter. Jumping on the spot. Laughter.

'Sorry! We're just so excited today, aren't we?'

'Come on, let's go in!'

'How much is it?'

'That's fifty bits, Ma'am.'

'Here you are. Thanks.'

RUN!

(Whisper) 'Are you awake?'

(me) 'Yes.' Feeling something in the belly. Tightness, like tension, but it's the good kind.

Hands on the body. Rolling it over. Body in bed. A smile. A kiss, soft. A kiss, a kiss, another kiss, each one harder than the last, more purposeful, more intense.

What's going on? I don't like this, I don't like feeling this way, I don't like being these people anymore! Get me out of here! I remember trying to jerk away but the body I was in was responding to the hands touching it, getting excited, and...

I can feel it in the belly, the growing excitement, breathing getting heavier, needs growing stronger, and *I'm too young for this, I'm not ready, this isn't what I want, my turn is being stolen from me, has been stolen from me, has gone!*

Gone.

I can never go back.

The body is straining, delighted, lips kissing, tongues licking, heart beating harder and faster as the bodies move to a rhythm; a beat I can't beat, it feels so incredible! And I hate it and love it and can't do anything but surrender to it. The body moves in desperate delight. I move in desperate delight. Yes. Yes. Yes! Yes! YES!

No.

With no warning I transition from delight to nothing. If whatever it is that makes me me could speak, had any inclination to form words, it would speak in monotone. It would communicate the blandest shade of grey. I have a memory, though, of the colour I was just in – my body is still tingling, I can still feel those organs (the ones I don't want to think about) engaged, and I'm not sure I can quite get my head around that because I've just started to get the hang of all this and I thought that when I move out of one expression and into another I was supposed to have forgotten what came before, I was supposed to be in the moment, I was supposed to be nothing but what I was forced to be. Through my link, my wrugs, I'm not supposed to remember what I just experienced, (what I just lost), at least not right now, while I'm still in the sim. I'm not supposed to even be aware of my simfulness; not until I get out. So what's going on?

But before I can pick the question apart, understand what's been happening a little more, I feel a sharp pain. A slice of blinding white. A stab, puncturing a hole in my stomach. A hot flood of blood. And for a moment I'm detached, still grey, but then GODDAMN IT! IT HURTS!

I look at my belly in surprise, expecting to see flesh peeled back, organs revealed, blood gushing, perhaps geyser like, like in the vids you know, or the books, or games, all those things where I could just imagine what it was like, rather than feeling it for real. But there's nothing wrong with my stomach, despite the pain. And the pain changes; it isn't hot anymore, or razor sharp; it's a hoof kick in the chest. POW! The wind is knocked out of me and I gulp and struggle to breathe. I look around, trying to see what kicked me, to figure out where I fell, to understand why I can't breathe anymore, but I'm just standing there, in a room, on my own.

I try to look at the room, but I can't focus on it; my eyes are blurring and I worry for a moment that I'm going blind, only I'm not. My eyes are blurring and my cheeks are wet and I understand that I'm crying. But I can't breathe, so I can't cry. Not really. Not the bawling kind, the kind that I want to do, the kind that fits the pain.

I struggle to pull air in, and the noise I make reminds me of this time when I was small and we went to the country to visit Granddad. We were out walking when I heard this strangled cry coming from the hedge in the garden. I was small and I pushed my way through the branches and leaves, not caring how they snagged my clothes and hair and skin, just fascinated by this gulping, wheezing, terror. And when I got through the hedge I saw a fox. Its head was twisted in the wire mesh of the fence that stood under the hedge. As I got closer the fox started to struggle, trying to get away, its eyes rolling as it looked at me, its instinct telling it to run. Only it couldn't. The wires were wrapped around its neck and the more it fought the more tangled it got. The wires squeezed its throat and as it tried to breathe this mournful, wheezing, choking, whine forced its way through its bared teeth. Its face was contorted in pain.

That's what I sound like. My chest is so tight and each breath is shuddering through my body. And then... the pressure lessens, air flows through in a whoosh and I'm screaming. SCREAMING! I fall to the floor and rock back and forth, trying to contain the fear, pain, anguish, sorrow that's running through me. I'm grieving.

Hang on a minute...

My granddad died before I was born. There's no such thing as 'countryside'. There are no foxes. There's nothing to see outside. Where am I? Am I misremembering everything?

'You look terrible,' someone says. I look up. It's my sister. Wait. Shut up. I don't have a sister! It's my sister.

I shrug and resume staring at the space in front of me.

'How long have you been like this?' she asks. What's her name? She's your sister, how can you forget her name? I don't have a sister. Mary-Ann. I shrug again.

'What do you care?'

'I don't. Mum asked me to check up on you. She said you haven't been answering your phone.'

'What does she care? Fuck off,' I whisper. 'FUCK OFF!'(*I don't like to swear!*)

And then I scream and run at her: intent to kill.

Come on! Wait... what am I talking about? What was I just doing?

Laughter bubbles up all over the room and there's a steady hum of voices, conversations progressing in perpetuity. The atmosphere is grand. This is a party.

See everyone enjoying themselves, talking to old friends, meeting strangers, friends of friends, people they've been introduced to because someone who knows them knows that there's something that links them to this person someone knows but they don't. And there's excitement because all of us, even us couples who are happily ensconced in our own private versions of family, are wondering what these encounters with these new people might bring us. Every new person you meet is an opportunity. A new chance for you to show your best self, the self you want to be. A chance to argue, or to agree, or to do both. A chance to love yourself more, to hate yourself more, to love or hate someone else more. A chance to feel. Another chance to be human. That's what meeting a new person is like. That's what a good party is like.

So, I have to ask myself, what is this little man in front of me giving me a chance to do? He won't stop talking. We've been 'talking' for fifteen minutes but I haven't said one word. He won't let me, he just runs on and on and on, and it isn't even interesting. Normally, when someone speaks about their passions it enthuses you too, even if it's something that totally isn't your thing. But, to be quite frank, I just don't give a shit about the small differences in the pigmentation of the leaves of different strains of dog rose. I don't care about the minute change in leaf shape and how it's virtually indiscernible. I didn't want a lecture. All I said was that the flowers he'd brought for Helen were particularly lovely. I don't know that I even thought they were lovely. I was just being polite, starting a conversation, putting him at ease. He'd looked so nervous. I was just being nice. But he won't stop talking now. And we aren't just talking about (and when I say 'we', I mean 'he') dog roses now; we've moved on to all sorts of wild roses. And then there's the various strains of domesticated roses, their histories, the techniques used to create hybrids, the pros and cons of hybrids, his personal favourite (the floribunda), competitions, the rose he's working on currently, the... I can't handle any more of this. What has he been giving me a chance to do? Pretend. And I've realised something: I don't like pretending.

'I'm sorry, Ambrose,' (of course his name is Ambrose!) 'but I have absolutely no interest in roses whatsoever. Good night.'

I leave him spluttering behind me. And I can't help but smile because, even though I was bored stiff, I really did get something out of that.

I got something out of that.

I get something out of that.

I get it.

I want it.

'I want you! I adore you! You're beautiful! I love the way you taste! I love the feel of your skin, its smell, its delicacy! Everything about you intoxicates me! Come down! Please! Bella donna! Come down to me, let me hold you in my arms, let me pepper you with tender kisses, let me worship you! If you do not come down I will surely die! I cannot live with—'

Wow! That was horrible. Who was that? Where am I? I can't see. I don't feel uncomfortable and yet I can't orientate myself. I can't tell up and down, I can't feel if I'm standing, sitting or lying down. I can't see anything. But, weirdly, I'm not scared.

6

haphazard, rash, ill-considered, ill-aimed, disturbed by excitement, (*a wild guess, shot, blow, venture; wild opinions, bowling*).

'This is it! I'm telling you. This. Is. It!'

'Mmm, what's it?'

'This!' A woman looms up in front of me waving a piece of paper in my face. I've never seen her before but of course I recognise her. She's my girlfriend. And who am I? I see my hands holding a book and I recognise them as mine yet they aren't *my* hands because I'm just a kid. And these hands belong to someone older. Someone whose hands are more delicate than mine, whose nails are longer, whose fingers are thinner. These hands belong to someone who has taken care of them. I remember (looking back at that moment now), that I sighed as I recognised my state of being and not being. It was like I'd been doing this for years and I was tired of it all – the pretence, the fighting against it, the need to absorb it all. Yes, I remember that

I sighed, but the outer me, the me that wasn't *me*, smiled at her indulgently. Of course. That was what I had been programmed to do at that moment. And I remember that, a moment later, I felt that smile deep inside; I loved her and wanted to look after her, and anything she found interesting I found fascinating because she was my other, my perfect half.

One of my lovely, delicate hands lets go of the book I'm holding and reaches out to grab the paper she's fluttering in my face. I look at it and of course it means nothing to me. I didn't expect anything else. It's just a scrawl of data.

'What is it?' I say, a laugh lurking under my words (not a mean laugh). I can tell she noticed the laugh, despite its best efforts to hide and she's trying to understand it but at the same time she's too excited to pay it enough mind and that's enough to make the laugh come out from under it all and dance a little in front of us. She knows it for what it is now (not a mean laugh at all) and she grins at me and I can feel myself melting with how much I love her.

'I've only gone and bloody done it!' she says.

And I feel excited. I feel terribly excited, like suddenly there's something running through my body that wants to get out, but I can't quite believe what she's saying and I think she can't mean she's done the whole thing. All she can mean is that she's had a bit of a breakthrough. She can't mean anything more than that, can she?

'What is it?' I say and I look at the paper – really look this time – *really* try to understand what she's given me. And I think I'm frowning and smiling at the same time, if that's possible (it isn't really).

She crouches down in front of me, takes the paper out of my hand and puts it down beside her. She takes the book out of my other hand and puts it down beside her.

She takes my hands in hers and looks at me. And it's a serious look, even though she's grinning.

'I found it,' she says. 'I've triple checked the data. I've looked at the specimens. I've done it. I've done it!'

I speak quietly because I don't quite believe this yet:

'You've worked it all out?'

She's nodding at me.

'I've done it! This is it!' she says and she picks up the paper again and flutters it in my face again and I take it again and look at it again and it all feels like it's happening for the first time. I look at it. I *really* look at it.

Jesus! It can't be... I look at it, *I* look at it, *me,* the real person, the kid, the one inside this woman that's crazy about this other woman. *I* look at it and I see what it is. It's the formula that changed everything. It's what we all learn about when we're just small and in playschool. It's the formula that means I don't get to sit on grass ever, and I don't have a grandfather in the countryside, and I've never seen a fox, and I don't enjoy the dirt, and I don't really know what roses smell like, and I've never seen a desert or an ass or the sea outside of a picture. It's the formula that made life as I know it, that forced us all into domed cities, barely connected with each other, separated by swathes of what we call 'unknown'. And I can't believe it.

'You've done it!' I say and I leap up and grab hold of her and I kiss her deep. I can feel her tongue against mine and it's the kind of feeling I know really well but *I* don't know it, because I've never kissed anyone like this before, I've never loved anyone like this.

LET ME OUT!

'You've done it!' I cry, full of joy but the real me is horrified because this is what we learn about all the time now: unintended consequences. I can feel their joy and hope and the reasons why what happened, happened, but I'm horrified because I know what comes later. I know how the world fell apart and how many people died and how difficult it was to rebuild anything at all.

'You've done it!' I cry and I think I'm going to burst with how happy I feel that she, my love, my life, has gone and done it and I couldn't be more proud. Those old fogeys she's worked under for the past year have been at this for aeons. And in she swoops and she gets it! She's done it! It took nothing, no time, none of the years for bitterness to grow – all we have here between us is hope and happiness – and I know, as I look at her, that nothing can go wrong. Nothing can go wrong!

LET ME OUT!

7

~ **boar,** tusked wild pig (*Sus scrofa*) from which domesticated pigs are descended; ~ **cat,** medium-sized wild feline, esp. European species (*Felis sylvestris*); ~ ' **cat** (fig.) hot-tempered or violent person; ~ ' cat *a.*, reckless, financially unsound, (of strike) sudden and UNOFFICIAL, (of well) drilled for oil etc. where there is only a possibility of success; ~ ' **fire,** = *Greek* FIRE1, will-o'-the-wisp, (fig.) thing that spreads rapidly; ~ ' **fowl,** game-bird(s); ~ **- goo'se chase,** foolish or hopeless or fruitless quest; ~ **horse,** horse not domesticated or broken in (' *horses would not drag* etc. *it from me,* **I** refuse to disclose the secret); *wild* HYACINTH ; ~ ' **life,** wild animals collectively; ~ **man,** (1) savage (2) political extremist; ~ *man of the woods,* orang-utan; *wild* OATS ; ~ **rice,** tall grass of genus *Zizania* yielding edible grains; ~ **silk,** silk from wild silkworms, or imitation of this from short silk fibres; *wild* THYME ; **W ~ West,** western US in time of lawlessness; ~ ' **wood,** (poet.) uncultivated or unfrequented woodland.

I could smell the musk of rutting stags. Stepping lightly, I moved toward the fence that marked the boundary of the field and the beginning of the forest. I could see the dried mud (churned up over years) that marked their jumping off point. And, sure enough, the freshest marks were barely an hour old.

I stood and listened. The breeze was useful (it hid my approach) but it made it difficult to hear them. So I strained to hear everything: leaves whispering past each other; trees complaining of old age, all creaks and moans; birds calling, finches, nuthatches, jays, thrush. I could hear the drilling of a woodpecker and the occasional call of crows. There are always crows. I heard the clicks and whirrs of insects. I heard leaves dropping, the season changing, the air cooling. I stood and listened and then I heard a step, a crack of wood, and the silence that follows when you know you've given yourself away. I listened and waited, holding my breath and hoping my heart wasn't too loud (because it doesn't matter how many times you do this, it's always exhilarating). I peered through the trees, into the gloom and tried to find the spot where that branch broke. Nothing moved. Of course. I stood, patient, still, ready to wait all evening if I had to.

Time slips forward, time melts, I melt, I am not myself, I'm nowhere I know and yet I know this place; I *am* this person and I've done this many times before, standing in the darkness, in the quiet, in the wild, listening, waiting, watching. I know the creature I heard is gone. It's time for me to go too, to move further into the dark, to move into the woodland, away from the fields and people and civilisation.

Strange. I shook my head. For a moment it had felt as if I wasn't myself. I looked around and noticed that the evening had grown much darker. I checked the time and was surprised. I had been standing there for over an hour. But I couldn't remember the time moving at all. I shrugged. The creature I had heard must have moved on by now. I stepped carefully, climbed over the fence, and moved as quietly as I could through the undergrowth. I crept forward, crouched down and I felt again as though there was someone else in my place, only this time I was there too, aware of it, but too far removed to panic. Together, we stalked. We heard a branch break. We froze. We turned our head towards the noise. A scream, a squeal, a roar, an explosion of sound and movement rushed at us. The other person in my head removed itself, it was just me and, running faster than my thoughts, a boar, head lowered, tusks sharp, ready to gore, pure fury in a body of solid muscle, moving fast, fast, too fast, intent to kill, and then...

This is a familiar feeling. I know this body. I've been here. No. It's slightly different. She said it was wild. She said: 'It's the ride of your life. Enjoy it!' My mind is stretching into the body of a cat – sinuous, simple, sun-soaked – and my thoughts are not really thoughts at all but impressions of things. I've done this before; I remember feeling this warmth. But it isn't like before. I'm not in that lazy frame of mind, observing the world as it rushes by me, apart from it. I mean, I do feel apart from it but it's different. For a start, I'm not lying on a hot stone slab. It's dark and I'm looking through the dark as if it were brighter than daylight. Cat's eyes. I have them. There's a lot out there and I want to see it all but I don't want any of it to see me. I'm sniffing the air, my body is tense, coiled tight, an engine, poised on the edge of performing anything, everything, something fast and strong and splendid.

I feel in control and wary and my stomach is soft and

full of expectation. I'm in charge, my actions are clear, purposeful; I'm on a mission.

I stretch into this cat and I walk, slinking, careful, silent, quick. I walk across a soft grassy lawn and smell the alien smell of it. This grass is lacking texture, definition. The earth beneath it is too dark, too rich, too fertile. And I can smell something strange and hard. Not rock, not like rock, it's baked hard, it's burnt, it fills my nose with fumes, but there, behind its nastiness... I smell oestrus. So, I step up to the dark rock that's not rock, this dark river of burnt bad smells. I step onto it and feel the hardness press beneath my pads, so stark, so hard compared with the softness of the grass. I run across it and onto another patch of bad grass. The oestrus smells stronger here, I can feel her close, I smell her, the feelings in my belly harden. Almost there. She brrrooos hello to me. I can hear her: small, soft, lazy, not right, not right but the smell of oestrus is strong. I flick my tail, thick, strong, powerful, and pause as I wonder: is it right, is it time? The smell of oestrus is strong.

I creep forwards. I can hear her. She brrrooos and she comes out of this strange solid mass. She paces up to me. She's small, so small! Not dark like me. She's white and grey and strange. Her fur is short, not thick like mine, not striped like mine, not strong like mine. She's small! She smells soft. She looks helpless. The oestrus is strong. I don't like her but I want her, this small, soft thing. We touch noses. I'm bending my head down low, she's so small. I nose around her, smell her around her anus. The smell of oestrus is strong. She's small but I mount her anyway. She's wrong but I mount her anyway. We yowl.

She yowled at me. I was so surprised by it I laughed and that's when she grabbed the lamp beside her and threw it across the room. I ducked but I wasn't fast enough. Luckily her aim wasn't perfect either and it just grazed my head before it fell to the ground behind me and broke.

'Jesus, Cath! Was that really necessary?'

I shouldn't have opened my mouth. Her face screwed up in fury; I've never seen a beautiful person look so bloody ugly. It made me shudder.

I shuddered and saw I was standing in an unfamiliar room, opposite an unfamiliar girl, and she looked really pissed off. I don't think I've ever seen anyone look that angry. I mean even my dad didn't look that angry when I tried to fly off of the balcony when I was six and I landed on the car and seriously damaged it with the armour I was wearing. He was furious then but I don't think he ever looked like this. I've read that expression about steam coming out of someone's ears – her face was so red I kind of expected to see something like that now. I kind of expected her head to explode. I was awestruck by the anger. I just stood there, not sure what to do. I didn't even think about the fact that I didn't know how I'd got there or who's house I was in or anything like that. I just remember that when I saw the girl I was too fascinated by her to think about much else. And I was so busy thinking about how her head was going to explode that I didn't notice her grabbing a remote control or something like that, (I don't know, it was black and had buttons on it and I remember seeing pictures of remote controls like that at school) and lobbing it at me. I didn't notice and I didn't move and the thing scythed through the air and hit me square in the eye and it hurt like a... I really want to say some pretty bad words, but I don't like swearing. And yeah – just like that:

'Cath – WHAT THE FUCK IS WRONG WITH YOU?'

The words are out of my mouth but I didn't know I'd even thought them and my voice was all wrong anyway and that was when it dawned on me that I was still in sim. This is when it got weirder. It felt like my mind had split into two. I was me *and* I was the guy I was right then. Truly aware in a way I hadn't been all the other times. I knew everything about this guy that I was that wasn't me: name, height, weight, blood type, national insurance number. I knew weird crap I don't even know about myself and I knew the angry girl was Catherine and she was my sister and I knew she was one crazy bitch (his words, not mine). I was clutching at my eye when she jumped at me and then it was a mess.

I've never been in a fight before, but this guy that I was had been in lots of fights, most of them with Cath. I was both in the moment and observing it and, for the first time in the sim, I didn't feel completely *in* the sim. I felt like I had some control. I didn't know what to do with it, though. So I just watched as me and Cath beat the crap out of each other. She had these long fingernails and she used them. I didn't know why she was angry but that wasn't strange. She was always taking offence at things that weren't designed to hurt her. She'd always been like that, ever since we were small. She was just so angry. And when she fought with me I could see it in her – the rage – and I felt helpless against it. It was this ever growing tide inside her and I didn't know where it came from or how to help her fight it down, and she looked so lost in it all that it made me want to cry. I couldn't help her, and I wanted to. I wanted to, so badly. She was all I had and I was all she had and we had to help each other. Didn't we? *Isn't that what being a family is about? Isn't there some way that I can make her happy? Isn't there some way?* She kicked out at me and I caught her leg and pulled it up. She went crashing down on her back and I heard her gasp as the wind burst out of her. I threw myself down on top of her and held tight. She struggled against me, fighting to get free, scrabbling with everything she had to get out of my grip and to keep going but I just held on as if my life depended on it. I held onto her and hoped she would calm down. I hoped she would let go. I hoped she would stop and talk to me. I held her and I began to cry. And after a while I noticed she was crying too. And she was holding onto me too. And we cried with each other.

'I'm not sure how to say this, so I'm just going to go ahead and say it–'

I shook my head almost violently at the words. The change was so sudden it left me reeling, as though I had just come out of a spin dryer or something. I was myself; I was Catherine's brother; and now I was... who? I knew exactly: I was a boy called Bobby. *Have I been this boy before? Wasn't I in a car, was I going to the water park?* I felt the same as I had that time; the body felt familiar. I was in a room, though, not a car, and even though I had just got there, I knew I had been there for a little while. Like I hadn't *just* got there as this boy, Bobby. Bobby had got there before me. *I* had just got there. So I was sitting in an office, next to my mum (who was holding Lilly), opposite a woman who had just said the words I wrote above, and I had just enough time in the pause, between the first clause of her sentence and the second, to think and feel everything I just wrote before she continued:

'Your husband lost all of your money through bad investments. Then he borrowed heavily to pay back what he lost... and he lost that too. You're seriously in debt.'

I don't understand what the woman is saying but I'm

angry with her because she's making Mum cry and Mum cries all the time anyway, so she doesn't need this woman to make her cry more. And it's worse because when Mum cries Lilly cries too, and she's starting now and she won't stop. Mum starts cuddling her and stroking her hair and saying:

'Sorry, baby girl. Don't cry! Everything's fine.'

But everything isn't fine because if it was we wouldn't all be crying. And the woman opposite is just shifting uncomfortably in her chair and she won't do anything to make it better and she just made it all worse so really she should be making it better. Shouldn't she?

I sigh and rub a hand over my forehead and, to stop myself from thinking about anything important, I focus on the rough feel of the skin beneath my fingertips. My forehead is ridged and lined. How did I get to be this old? Where did the years go? But I know where the years went; I'm asking these questions just as a distraction, to stop myself from looking at the numbers in front of me. Lots of numbers. And none of them mine. And I can't quite get my head around the reality of the situation because none of it has really been real, has it? Numbers aren't real; they're just marks on a piece of paper, pixels on a screen. They're imaginary. And yes, they make sense, but they aren't *real*. So these numbers in front of me mean nothing. Only they do mean something. I can't quite figure out how these imaginary things relate to the real material objects around me but I lost a lot of imaginary numbers and now all of the other stuff I have, the real stuff, is going to be lost too. There's something I can do. I'm sure there's something I can do to fix this. What's that guy's name again? The one I met at that party, a month ago? I got the impression that he was willing to loan out numbers. He has them spare... Carl! Carl Stevenson. I have his card somewhere, I can call him. I bet he could loan me some numbers to help tide me over until I win some back, right? I should find his card. I reckon he'll help. I ought to call him. I sigh and rub a hand over my forehead. I feel so goddamn nervous! My stomach is crawling insects and I'm light-headed. I can't sit still, but when I stand up I feel like I'm going to fall over. But I know if I sort out these numbers I'll feel better. I'll be squared away. I have to find that card, give Carl Stevenson a call. I just need a few more numbers to make the landscape work properly again. That'll make it fine. I ought to find that card. Give Carl Stevenson a call.

I don't know about this. I'm shaking my head. I don't think this is a good idea. I mean, we should tell someone, right? We can't just do it, we can't just stop working.

But just stopping is the point! That's what Sally keeps saying. We need to make a statement! (She seems to speak in exclamations.) See, they don't understand now, do they? Those people up at the top – they don't realise how much they rely on us. They don't realise how much we do! This is old news to them, routine, just part of every day. It isn't critical anymore because we've got a handle on it. Don't you see! *We* have got a handle on it. But they think they're included in that *we*. They think they're in charge. But *we* have the power! *Us!* They need us, not the other way around! We are the frontline! We're the ones saving lives! And yet, despite everything, they don't seem to think that we're entitled to adequate protection. And we've tried talking to them. So now we have to just stop! It's down to us to make the point. *We* have to make a statement! No one else is going to make it for us!

That's what Sally said. And I know I felt sure at the time. She was *so* right, wasn't she? I felt infected with her passion. I'd never felt so certain about anything. *Yes!* I thought. *Yes!* But I don't know anymore. Because if we just stop, well, there are consequences. Sally said that was the point; the consequences are the statement. The consequences are the proof. But I don't know if I can live with them. I mean could you? Could you live with them?

Wait, is she asking me? Does she know that I'm here, inside her body? Does she know that I'm experiencing everything with her? Is she even a real person in the same way that – Oh god! I was there wasn't I? When Lilly Emerson discovered the formula. I was there, right? That was the moment. And Lilly Emerson is real as real can be. So this woman I'm in right now, is she real too? Is everyone real? I remember I was a rose. I was a rose! Is this woman asking me what I think? Is she talking to me?

Could you live knowing that you were responsible for people dying? Because people will die. Those people up at the top, the ones Sally says have to pay, they won't just give us what we want straight away; they won't give us the support we need to safely help the infected. People have to die first. A lot of people. Because those guys are going to wait to see if we can handle the consequences; they're going to expect us to give in before they do. They're hard. That's why they're up there and we're down here. That's what I reckon. So, I don't know about this.

'You coming, Luce?' Tom asks me.

'I don't know about this,' I say. 'Are you sure about this?' I turn and ask Greg.

Greg doesn't answer straight away.

'No. I'm not. Are you coming?' he asks and he holds out his hand to me.

No! What am I feeling? I'm not one of them right now, am I? I can't tell. Sally. Sally. We learned about a Sally Pardew at school. Is this it? Is this that time? Am I one of the people she convinced to stop that day? Am I–

It is getting to be real boring hearing people say they think I'm crazy. I don't think they understand what 'crazy' really means. I think the best word to describe me is 'hopeful'. I've a feeling. My momma always said I had good instincts. As a child I never seemed to get it wrong. I could tell about things. And that didn't go away as I grew up. People have seen the fruits of my instincts before now so why they think I'm crazy really beats me. I've not been wrong yet. Why do they think this time is any different? Because no one else is doing what I'm doing? I sometimes wonder how people think anything gets created, innovated, developed, evolved. I know, as sure as the rocks beneath my feet, that when I come up with the goods they'll all be saying they knew I was right all along. And they'll not bat an eyelid. That kind of shamelessness staggers me. My momma said it was because I never did understand the art of lying.

'You tell it how it is, son, even when no words is fine. Sometimes I wish you never knew how to use that tongue of your'n.'

I suppose I never really understood the best time not to say something. I'm better at that now. I keep myself to myself. And that's easy to do up here. I only have the earth for company, and I can feel her talking to me. She don't lie like folks do. I don't believe many people understand her when she speaks, but I have the feel for it. She told me to come up here. She told me this was where it was. I trust her in a way I won't never trust a person. I've been hiking around these parts for a few days now and I can feel that

I'm close. I do believe I am on the verge of finding what she wants to give me. She's coy about it, she wants me to do some work, but of course you've always got to work for things that are worth having, don't you? I wouldn't trust her half so much if she gave up the goods at the tip of my hat. Pretty soon folks ain't going to be calling me crazy. Which is good because it is getting real boring to hear them call me crazy.

I take a deep breath and smell that rich conifer perfume. The rocks press into the soles of my shoes. It hasn't rained for a good while now and the air is dusty. A fly buzzes. *Everything feels untouched.* Well, of course it feels untouched! No one has touched it. *But this kind of land, it doesn't exist does it?* Well, I am standing on it aren't I?! *This isn't real*, of course it's real, *it isn't true, I'm not really here, what's happening?* I just want to listen to the earth, who are you, why are you questioning me? *Can he hear me? Who is he,* who are you, are you me, *am I still here*, are you real, *is he real?*

I panic. I panicked. I was panicking.

My mother told me not to linger. But I had to see him, didn't I? He had to ask me to dance. I had to say yes. We had to take a walk, get some air. He had to hold my hand. I had to like it, to want more. I had to linger. Oh God, it was lovely! And now it's dark. I didn't even notice the time pass, didn't realise until it was night; it was so lovely!

Bloody hell. She's going to be furious. I hate this stretch, it gives me the willies. Even in daylight, there's something about this stretch of land... God, and it smells! I wish I could see better. She's going to murder me, she'll kill me where I stand; I'll die. I won't even get into the house. I can just hear her now: 'I've a mind to skin you, Jessie! I'll tan your hide, I will!' And she will so. I reckon she was hoping, secretly, that I wouldn't come home on time. God, I *hate* this stretch of land! Why, in hell, do we live on the other side of it? Jesus. I shouldn't blaspheme so much. God, this place gives me the creeps. Jesus! Crap, I can't seem to leave the Almighty alone! I wish I could see better. Silly goose, it's not that bad out here. Let's think nice things, get us through, right? Daniel, let's think about Daniel. Has there ever been such a beautiful lad in all the world? And he wanted me to dance with him. *Me*! I don't really care if she does skin me; he's worth it. And he was such the gentleman when he – hang on, is that a light? Thank God! Hang on, wait, I *bet* she's coming to find me. I can't believe her! As if I haven't lived here all my life, as if I don't know my way home. What does she think is going to happen to me out here?

'Mam! I'm coming! You didn't have to come out here in this chill just to find me, I can find my way!'

Though I have to admit, it is nice to have a light close by. I know it's silly, but this place really does give me the creeps. Wait...

'Hey! Where are you going? I'm over here! Oh, come on! Now that you've come all this way you may as well help me home! Come on, I'm sorry! Mam!'

Jesus, now I have to run after her! She's awful. I can't believe she would be so petty; she's worse than a child. I swear, when I have one of my own...

'Wait for me!'

How is she moving so fast? She loves making me work. This is all part of her punishment. I swear to God when I marry Daniel I'll *not* bother making this journey to see her, I can tell you that much for free, I–

'Whooaah! God, that was close. Nearly fell over Jessie, my dear, you ought to be more careful as you go. I didn't realise how muddy it was around here. Great, and now I'm talking out loud to myself. Well, it breaks up the quiet now, doesn't it? And it's not as if there's anyone out here to hear me. May as well keep talking; it's not like she – where's the light gone? Mam? Mam! Where are you? Come on! This isn't funny! Come back! I–'

Oh my... why won't my leg move? Come on Jessie, pull. Pull harder. Come on pull. Pull! PULL! Oh God.

Oh God, oh God, oh God, oh God, oh God! Come on Jessie, pull; you can get out of here.

'MAM! MAMMY, I'M STUCK! CAN YOU COME AND GET ME? I THINK I'M STUCK IN THE BOG. I CAN'T GET MY LEG OUT. MAM! *Mam*! Mam? I can't get my leg out. Or my other leg. I'm stuck, Mammy.'

No one's coming. I shouldn't have lingered. Mam told me not to linger. And then night came so quick. I couldn't see. How could I be so stupid? I grew up around here. I should know, I should *know*! Why didn't she come the whole way? She came out to find me, why didn't she come the whole way? She did come out to find me, didn't she? Oh God, that wasn't... I completely messed up, didn't I? How could I be so bloody stupid? She always said to be mindful of the marsh lights. Of course she didn't come out to find me. She'd expect me to know better than to be tricked by a wisp. And no one's coming now. Don't cry, Jessie, don't cry. Oh for Christ's sake! What good will crying do!? No one's coming are they? Oh God, I'm sinking!

This is it, isn't it? She told me not to linger, but I had to see him, didn't I? Well, Jessie, was he worth it? Your beautiful boy, was he worth it? God. I'm sorry. I'm sinking pretty slowly. Maybe I'll still be here in the morning. Maybe someone'll reach me before my head goes under? Maybe? Jesus, it reeks, how did I not notice I was wandering right into it? I was so full up on everything else, stupid girl! This is it – the end of Jessie Wilkes, flirt and airhead, drowned in a bog. This is it. This is it, isn't it? This is it. Jesus, that smell! Well, let's think about it all then. I have time, I don't need a flash, I can see my whole life at leisure. Let's look back.

I feel cold. The air is so cold! But my legs are warm. I guess a bog is good for something. At least I won't freeze to death. Oop, it's reached my waist. I didn't think it would rise this fast, I mean I didn't think I would sink this fast, am I sinking fast or did I just... disappear, for a while?

God, it really is warm in here! It's like sinking into hell, I guess. Have I been good enough? It's at my neck. It's at my neck. I've tried to be good, I think. I have been good, haven't I? I blaspheme too much, but I love Our Lord. I try to do the right thing. I've been hard on Mam, but I've tried, haven't I? Am I just imagining it all? Am I really bad? Oh God, the smell! Eugh, the taste! Why, oh Christ, why did I open my mouth just then? Eugh! It tastes worse than it smells. What is that smell?

I've never smelled anything like it. I smell it every day but I have never smelled anything like it. Because I'm about to die? Or because I'm not really me? The black muck starts to ooze into my nostrils and I know pretty soon I'll start to drown. The smell fills me up and as it does I rise out and I see Jessie down below, trapped in the bog, not struggling, just sinking, and I watch her dying, and I know every thought she has in her head; I know the panic she's feeling, and it feels like the body I don't have is flooded with that lightness you get when you're so afraid it's as if you almost aren't there anymore, and

I can't breathe either. The smell is filling me up and as I struggle and die I find myself removed from one body to another, and to another, and to another, and all I'm getting is fragments of thoughts and parts of speech, and I'm not following it but I'm getting the sense these fragments make a whole. I jump.

'I have a report to make – this thing, it's... just get Dr Shapiro here soon. She's going to want to see it for herself.'

'Did you hear about what it did to that junior lab assistant?'

'Dr Shapiro didn't come to work today. You don't think–'

'–We need to keep this thing quiet. We don't need the kind of mass panic we got after the–'

'–I think there's something going on there and I'm scared. You can't tell anyone what I've told you, I really think... I think someone might–'

'–No members of staff at the University are willing to discuss the chain of events that have led to such drastic action, but the chancellor has confirmed the rumour that the institution is closing its doors indefinitely. In the absence of an official statement, our investigator went to talk to some of the students who are effectively being prevented from completing the further education they have paid for–'

'–It's important for everyone to remain calm. This evacuation is merely for preventative purposes. It will not be long before you can return to your homes but for now we ask you to pack only a few items in a bag that does not exceed–'

'–It has been confirmed that Bolton is now under quarantine. This is the third city in the last week that has officially been quarantined, bringing the total up to seven.

The mayor has made a statement–'

'–I have something to tell you. It wasn't Dr Shapiro–'

'–It's hard to say what really happened.'

'What d'you mean? You know what happened?'

'Everyone is saying that Dr Shapiro planned this.'

'I've never heard such bullshit in my life! Why would the whole lab go along with that, you're–'

'–Will you stop with the conspiracy theories! Everyone knows what happened; it was made pretty clear when they–'

'–What are you talking about? What's Lilly got to do with this?'

'Did you hear about Lilly and Shapiro?'

'We tried to talk to Ms Emerson's mother but she declined to–'

'–Bobby just went mad at them. Did you see that video on the–'

'–I remember them when they were kids, poor wee tykes, losing their father so young, it was–'

'–Calm down, Bobby, I can't–'

'–And in our headlines today: Charlie Roberts makes a statement about his relationship, and that of his late sister, Catherine Roberts, with Lilly Emerson.'

'Did you hear what Charlie Roberts had to say about Lilly? I can't believe–'

'–And what was that thing about Dr Shapiro? The whole thing has been an absolute disaster.'

'Yes, everyone's ready to blame Lilly, just like they were all ready to blame Shapiro before that. Who's next? Cath Roberts? Charlie? Bobby Emerson? The blame game is no different from a virus; there's–'

'–I know. I was there when the news came out right after she–'

'–You were cheering like everyone else! You should feel ashamed of yourself.'

'People are dying out there!'

'It's been seventeen days since our last fatality, and–'

'–We are putting new protocols into place to prevent anything like this happening again. A detailed list of–'

'–Have you seen these rules we have to adhere to now? I can't believe this, it's like–'

I feel such hatred and fear as I jump, but I feel something else too: excitement. People are on fire with the stories. They love it. They love hating and feeling scared; they love making their emotions look greater than they feel. *I* love it. I love the attention, I love to talk. I want to tell everyone what *I* am thinking because I'm more important than them, my opinions count for more, I've been hurt more, I've suffered more, I've done it with more grace and more integrity, I'm better than you, I'm just so important! And I'm above the judgements of others. I'm the judge. I know who to blame, who to complain about, I know who's at fault.

I breathe, gulping air as if it's water. I feel like I need to purge myself of everything I've just taken in, fill myself up with fresh air, air that doesn't taste like bog muck, or bullshit. I'm shaking with the sanctimonious rage of the masses. I'm so full of hate and I'm trying to expel it because this isn't *me*. I don't hate like this. I don't know how a body can contain emotion like this – so big and violent, and hard! And I–

'Eeehuuuuuuh!' I gulped in air by the gallon as I sat up, looking around blindly, feeling like I'd fallen a long way down.

'Ssh!' a voice hissed and I turned around to look.

A man was crouched down in the grass behind me.

Grass! Wait. I've seen this before!

'Where am I?'

'Shut up!' the man whispered.

I've been here before! I was in this grass and this guy...

The man crept forwards until he was next to me. He was holding a rifle. I'd never seen a rifle in real life before but I knew what it was. I'd seen one like this in the old museum, and I'd seen them in classic vids. And of course there were the little wooden pistols my mum gave me. I felt excited, not just because I recognised this moment but because now, going back to it, I could pay more attention. I was out in the open, in the grass! There was a blue sky above me and the man had a dog. A dog! I looked around for it.

The man glared at me before creeping ahead. In his wake, crawling on its belly, was the dog I was looking for. I had forgotten how vicious he looked. People used to keep those things. Looking at him, I don't get why.

The dog didn't notice me; it just crawled on after the man. Last time I was here I tried to follow them, but not this time. I knew what was going to happen. Instead, I looked at everything. Ahead of us, and all around, were small groups of trees. I think people used to call them copses. I remember reading the word in a book, one of those heavy, old-fashioned types we're made to read in history class. The air was crisp and frosty. It felt like the kind of winter you read about. Not that anyone's experienced a real season in forever. That's the cool thing about enclosed cities – total climate control. I sniffed. It smelled so unfamiliar to me and yet my brain was filling in the names of the scents anyway – leaf mould, dew, manure, haylage – it was a farmy, outdoorsy smell, and I didn't know how I knew it. I also didn't know how I could be myself here when, for the most part, I had been other people. I was trying to see the pattern of what had gone before but I just couldn't work it out.

'PEHKUUUUUUUUUUUUUUUUUUK!'

A bird exploded into the air, making me jump, just like the last time. My heart raced from the fright but my eyes were up, watching it fly; it was extraordinarily beautiful. I didn't get a chance to appreciate that the time before.

'BANG!'

I jumped again, even though I knew it was coming. I heard the dog bark and the man shout out.

'Did you see that?' The man shouted. 'That's how it's done.'

I blinked and looked up at the empty sky.

But the sky wasn't empty; branches stretched up into it, leaves covered it up, lapping and overlapping each other, occasionally riffling aside in the breeze to reveal the blue I had been looking at.

I knew this would be brilliant! Time with Lucy is always the best. I just knew her birthday would be brilliant!

'Listen carefully, everyone,' says Lucy's dad. 'Snipe are very shy. They don't like to come out in the day, so they hide in pretty dark places. You should concentrate on cracks in rocks, hollow trees, pools, even puddles of water. They like sharp, rhythmic noises; hitting two sticks together, or possibly two rocks, simulates mothering calls and these noises may draw snipe to you, so make sure you keep it up. Okay! Who's ready to hunt some snipe?!'

'Mr Seger?'

Paul's put up his hand.

'Yeah?'

'What exactly do snipe look like? I know they're birds, but what if we catch the wrong bird?'

'Good question! Snipe don't look like most birds. This is because they're flightless, which is what makes them easy for us to catch. They have very small wings and they aren't feathered, but covered in black skin. Some snipe – not all, mind – are amphibious. Hands up who knows what amphibious means... yeah, Sara?'

'They're like frogs, aren't they?'

'Bingo!' (I grin happily at being right) 'Amphibious means that they can live both in water and on land. That's why you have to make sure you look in some of the pools. But, health warning guys: be careful around the water! Are you ready to–'

'–Billy, I think we need to give them a few more health warnings,' says Lucy's mum.

'Like?' Lucy's dad drags out the 'i' in 'like' so it's more like: liiiiiiike. (A fat 'i' should go there – one that spreads over the space instead of lots of little thin 'i's that make the word look like it's stuttering.)

'Kids, be careful if you find any cracks in the rocks and things. You can look in them, but remember snakes like to make dark small spaces like that their homes too. The snakes here aren't dangerous but they still might bite.'

'Oh, right, yeah, the snakes!' says Lucy's dad and he smiles like he's embarrassed. 'Be careful of snakes, everyone!'

I look at Lucy's mum. She's smiling at Lucy's dad like she's forgotten there's anyone else alive. They both look really happy. I look at Lucy. She looks happy too. It's her birthday so you expect her to look happy, but I think she's happy most days. She never has a bad word to say about anyone. Lucy's cool.

'Okay – ready to hunt some snipe?'

'YEAH!' we all shout together.

'On the count of three: One – Two – Three!'

Run! Run Sara, run! This is so exciting! Where's Lucy? I want to stick with Lucy.

'Lucy!' I shout.

'Yeah?'

'Let's hunt together!'

'Yeah!'

We hold hands and run.

'I know where we should start,' says Lucy. 'There's a pool a ways in. Dad took me there before.'

'Have you ever caught a snipe before, Lucy?'

Lucy shakes her head.

'Dad's told me about them, but we've never been hunting. He said we'd go when I was older. I guess I'm older!'

I nod and I'm so happy because this means I'm older too and it feels as though I've been let in on some big secret, that I'm part of some club. It's a warm feeling and it spreads through me so my body feels like it's humming.

Lucy pulls me further into the woods, where it's darker. The trees are closer together, the leaves cover the sky. It's quieter. I can't hear the other kids so much here, just a shout now and again, a squeal, a giggle, but they're distant. Lucy's hand is clammy in mine, so I let go. She pushes on ahead of me, through some plants.

'Come on, Sara,' she whispers. 'It's through here. We have to be real quiet.'

I hold my breath. My heart is beating faster and I'm sure that we're going to find a snipe here, even though it's only the first place we're looking; even though they're hard to catch, I'm sure that we're the lucky ones. Lucy disappears into a screen of green. I push after her, worried for a moment that I'm going to lose her, and find myself in a small clearing. Straight up is clear blue sky. Ahead of me, Lucy is kneeling on a rock beside a little pool of water.

'Come look,' Lucy whispers, waving me over.

I creep over to the pool side and kneel down next to her. We look into the pool. It's dark, murky, a skin of green stuff covers its surface. It looks gross.

'Isn't it awesome!?' Lucy says.

I think it looks disgusting, but I want to be cool like Lucy so I just nod and smile at her.

'Look! Look, you can see tadpoles in there.'

This makes me much more interested. I like tadpoles. They turn into frogs and I really like frogs. I think they're pretty cute. But I've never seen a real one, or a real tadpole either. I asked my parents once if we could get a pond at home but they said no and soon after that they sold our garden. I decide the pool isn't disgusting anymore. I look closer and, sure enough, drifting amongst the browns and greens (murky colours that make the pool look like a dark eye) are little tadpoles. I don't see anything snipe-like, though.

'Hey Lucy, shouldn't we be hitting sticks together? Your dad said something about making noises.'

'Oh yeah! I forgot.'

I grin, happy to have been useful, to have remembered something important that Lucy forgot. I feel like I might be a bit smarter than her, (after all, I knew what amphibious meant, too), but then I guess she brought me to the pool so maybe we're evens.

'Here,' Lucy hands me some rocks and I start clacking them against each other.

'No Sara, you're hitting them together too fast. It should be a steady beat, like this.' Lucy hits her rocks together:

Clack --- clack --- clack --- clack --- clack --- clack.

I join in, trying to hit mine at the same time as her:

Clack --- clack --- clack --- clack --- clack --- clack ---

We hit our rocks together in time and sit by the pool for what feels like ages. I lose concentration, I'm not looking around for snipe anymore. I'm just listening to the clacking rocks. I almost feel like I'm sleeping. Then the sound changes. Lucy scrapes her rocks together and stops and looks at me. I shake my head, and focus again.

'I don't think there're any snipe here,' Lucy says.

'Should we go look somewhere else?'

Lucy nods: 'I know another place.'

We walk through the woods, clacking our rocks as we go, stepping carefully, trying not to disturb the undergrowth, the leaf litter, the sticks. I'm trying not to breathe, even – just to clack my rocks, because I believe this is going to bring the snipe out. We are so engrossed in our task that we don't hear the calls at first. But finally, Lucy breaks the spell, breaks our rock rhythm again:

'Sara, can you hear that?'

I stop clacking and listen.

'Lucy!' I hear. 'Lucy! Sara! Luuuuuucy!' It's Lucy's dad. (He drags out the 'u' in Lucy; it should be a fat 'u', fatter than an 'o'.) I look around then.

'It's almost dark!' I say. I see Lucy shiver.

'That's dad,' she says. 'I wonder if anyone else caught a snipe.'

'I hope not,' I say, all serious. Lucy giggles.

'Me too!'

'Luuuuuuuucy!' Lucy's dad calls.

'Guess we should try and find him!' says Lucy. She holds out her hand. I drop my rocks and take it. We start running and suddenly I don't care that we didn't find any snipe. We're hunters! And this wood is *our* world. We run towards Lucy's dad's voice. His calls of 'Luuuuuucy' and 'Saaaaaaaara!' get louder. Then we break through the undergrowth, hit daylight (less bright than before), and hit Lucy's dad. We're breathless and giggling. Lucy's dad's frown melts into a smile.

'Lucy! Thank goodness. We thought you'd been abducted by aliens!'

We burst out laughing at this.

'Don't be silly; aliens don't come in the daytime! We were just snipe hunting.'

'Oh! Oh I see... I didn't realise aliens were so particular about the scheduling of their abductions. Did you catch anything?'

I frown and Lucy says:

'No. We were clacking our rocks together for aaaaaaaages,' (she drags out the 'a' just like her dad!) 'but nothing came.'

'I was so sure we would find them. We went to all the right kinds of places,' I say. 'And we were so quiet and we just kept clacking, and we clacked them right, I know we did!'

Lucy's dad looks at me and I'm not sure why but he starts laughing.

'Better luck next time, Sara, hey?'

'You mean we get to do this again?' I ask him.

'Of course we can! Why wouldn't we?'

'It's just that Mum and Dad don't bring me out here. They say we shouldn't be going anywhere near nature anymore. They say it's been ruined, you know.'

Lucy's dad suddenly looks worried.

'Sara, did you tell Jules about what your parents think about the woods?'

I shake my head.

'No, Mr Seger, why would I?'

Suddenly Lucy's dad grips my hand and he pulls me away from the edge of the woods. He drags me over to Lucy's mum.

'Mr Seger! Ow, you're pulling too hard.'

Lucy's dad let's go of my hand.

'Dad?' Lucy says.

'Sorry,' he says, but he doesn't say it like he means it. 'Jules!' he snaps and I wonder why he's suddenly mad at Lucy's mum. 'Jules, we need to get Sara home, now.'

I'm starting to feel really scared.

'Why, Mr Seger? I thought we were camping out here.'

'What's going on, Billy?

'Sara just told me her parents don't usually bring her out like this.' Lucy's dad says this in a really strange way, like he's really saying something else.

'Mr Seger?' I ask, but he ignores me. Lucy's mum looks down at me and her brow is furrowed so her face is all worried.

'Is that true, Sara? Your parents don't like you out in the woods?'

I nod and she sighs like she's suddenly really tired and sad.

'Why didn't you tell us sooner, Sara?'

I shrug.

'I wanted to come out snipe hunting. And I wanted to see the woods. I've never seen the woods outside of the pictures before, and I've never seen real tadpoles. I saw some real tadpoles today!' I say it kind of desperately because I'm suddenly really scared that they're angry at me and I want them to know how important coming out today was to me. 'I really like frogs,' I say. 'I really wanted to come out. Please don't be angry with me. I didn't know I was supposed to tell you. I didn't know!'

'Shh,' Lucy's mum says and she hugs me. It surprises me. I wasn't expecting it. 'We're not angry with you, Sara, but I think you *did* know that you should have told us how your parents feel about the woods.'

I start to cry because she's right; I knew I should have told them.

'I just wanted to see a snipe,' I say. Then I hear Paul laughing.

'She's so stupid,' he says. 'Everyone knows that the snipe aren't real. It was just a *game*!'

'Shut up!' Lucy says in a fierce whisper.

I feel like my stomach has disappeared. I'm light inside, empty. I'm not crying anymore but I keep my face buried in Lucy's mum's stomach and I pretend I didn't hear anything. I would rather pretend, but I feel so stupid. So terribly, terribly stupid.

Sara isn't crying but I'm crying so hard I feel like I might break apart. I feel like I've lost something really important and it's the kind of thing that if you lose it there isn't a chance to get it back again. Not if you want to stay who you are. I'm crying but I don't want to. I don't want to feel this way. I want to stop, so I pull away from Jules, Mrs Seger, Lucy's mum, only that woman I was just hugging isn't what I'm pulling away from at all. I'm pushing myself up from the ground and I'm alone in a landscape so beautiful it doesn't stop me crying. I've seen something like this. It was different but it had the same feeling: empty but alive. I was walking on a mountainside, and listening to the earth. But I am not that man; this time I'm myself and I feel more myself than I have before. Only I'm different, aren't I? There's something different about me, I–

Come on, focus. I lie down on the top of the bluff and look out over a flat expanse of grass, empty, though in the distance there are mountains. I lie there and take it all in. A sharp breeze is gusting, and the grassland below me shivers under it. The air smells of cold and green and dry dust. On a rock, near my elbow, I spot a grasshopper, its body casing black and ochre. I watch it for a long time, absorbed in the occasional flicker of its antennae, waiting for it to jump. And then I hear them. Before I have time to look up I feel as though I'm lurching, like I've been lifted up by something and I'm being dragged awkwardly through the air, only I can't see anything, no up or down, earth or air. I wonder if this is because my eyes are closed, so I open them.

I breathe in deep, my thick lips rippling against each other, rumbling a whicker. My barrel belly narrows and then swells. I bend my head down, the muscles in my thick neck rippling as I move. I feel everything in my body. I'm aware of everything around me even as I lower my head and crop at the green. She comes to me, nudges into my belly, breathes lightly onto my side, and I feel the soft velvet of her lips as they caress my underbelly before she clamps them around my nipple and pulls at the milk. Tug, tug, tug. I can hear the milk and the swallow of her throat. I listen to the breeze. I listen to the other mares crop. I listen to him suckle at her, and her suckle at her, and him crop and him crop. I listen to the breeze and the tug and suckle and pull, the steady crop, the sighs. I hear him moving, restless, keeping his eye out for everything. I listen to it all, body tense, ready for anything at any moment, and yet I feel content. I crop at the green, enjoy its bitter juice. I flick my tail and listen and smell and taste and look and listen.

I blink and I'm myself, though my mouth feels sticky and sour. I remember being not myself now, I remember being something else: solid, calm and quiet. I feel solid, calm and quiet. And I'm not myself.

I'm nervous and I keep swallowing and tugging at the skirt of my dress. It's too short. I shouldn't have worn it. Why did I wear it? I wanted to impress him, didn't I. Stupid. Why would a dress that's a stupid length be impressive? I hope it takes more to impress him than that, otherwise what the hell am I doing here? He's late, isn't he; that isn't a good sign. He's late. Shit, no, I'm just early, like a goddamn idiot.

Oh, thank God, there he is. Smile. No, not like that, smile like you aren't terrified!

'Hi! I didn't expect you to be here already. I hope you weren't waiting long?'

Oh God, he thinks I'm a total loser for coming this early, doesn't he?

'No, not at all, I literally just arrived.'

Good, that didn't sound too much like a lie, did it? Bright smile. He looks good, nice shirt, mmm nice smell too, oh shut up, focus, sit.

'You look great!' he says. Liar. I look like an eejit.

'Thanks, you don't look so bad yourself!' Christ, bad line, how predictable, what's wrong with me? 'Sorry. I haven't been on a date in a while. I'm kind of rusty so try not to judge me on any clichéd statements I might come out with.' *Why* am I explaining myself? I'm only making it worse – oh God, he's smiling and I can't tell if it's one of those 'oh you poor pathetic loser' kind of smiles, or if it's a 'wow, what a mistake coming here, let's smile and pretend none of this is happening' kind of smile.

'Well, despite my dashing good looks, I don't actually

go on many dates myself, so rest assured you'll be matched cliché for cliché.'

Laugh. Laugh a little, make it look like you at least found that line a little bit funny. Is he really unfunny? Did I agree to go on a date with someone really unfunny? Is this just his way of dealing with disappointment?

'God, that was a terrible joke. I'm nervous. Look, there's no pressure here. Let's just pretend we're two mates having dinner and see how the rest goes.'

'The rest?'

He's gone a bit red!

'By 'rest', I just mean the conversation!'

'Oh. *That's* what you mean, is it?'

He's smiling now and I feel better too. Maybe this won't be a total wreck. Ooh, menus! It's like a switch has been flicked: we relax and conversation flies back and forth. Banter, how's the food, should we get more wine, what did you think of that recent paper, talk about the faculty, jokes about the faculty, gossip, where have you lived before, when did you get here? I glide over the easy topics and deal with the hard ones with well-rehearsed answers. But it happens, of course: he takes a logical conversational step and asks the questions I can't answer smoothly, because I still care too much. He asks:

'So what did your parents do?'

My smile stays on my face but I feel it changing, no longer elastic, but brittle.

'Mum was a writer. A journalist to start with but then she started writing books. Non-fiction, history stuff.'

'And your father?'

'Never had one.'

He looks at me and I feel I have to explain: 'Mum was a lesbian.'

'Did you have another mother?'

'No.' My voice is brittle too.

'Oh.'

He's searching for more to say, and I think he thinks that I'm ashamed of mum, that I'm embarrassed, but of course I'm not. I just can't tell him the truth – that I did have two mothers and one of them was Lilly Emerson. I can never tell anyone that. I don't want to hear their awkward, backtracking platitudes; the kinds of things people say when they don't want to say anything bad to your face. Or maybe he's one of those that actually would say something bad to my face? No. I don't think so. But I don't want to see that look on his face, that 'oh shit' look; the one that says he has no idea how to talk to me anymore because I'm no longer myself but Lilly Emerson's daughter. As if her personality supersedes mine, drowns me out, takes over my body in some way. It isn't fair. I can't tell him any of that. I can never tell anyone. I know this is a fact.

'Should I ask for the bill?' he asks.

I nod and feel a little sad.

I nod, I nod, I nod, I nod, I nod, I nod, I nod, I nod, I nod, I nod, I nod, I nod, I nod my thirteen heads in the breeze, we bounce a little up and down in the shade of the hazel tree, I heard it called by a creature that spoke too loud, I fear it near trod on me, and I don't know how I know it spoke, but know I do and as it spoke I nod, nod, nodded in agreement, in understanding, I knew, I knew what it said, I knew what I was and they called me the hyacinth girl! I nod, I nod, I know, I know, I agree, I know, yes it's true little wind, yes it's true hazel, it's true, I know, I nod, it's true, it's me, they called me the hyacinth girl... I feel so soft and sad in the wind, I know

I shan't live long, I nod at you and you and you, and I know I can't live long and yet I shall, I will, I do! I am perpetual! I live! But look at me, my many heads, so gently nodding, so sweet and sad and you look at me, you do, and you and you and you too, and you long to pick me up, tear me up, turn me into something I am not, I am not that thing, I am not it, I nod, I agree, I am not it, but only me! Look, they called me the hyacinth girl, I heard them say it and I nodded. I nod, I nod, I nod, I nod, I nod, I nod, I nod, I nod, I nod, I nod, I nod, I nod, I nod my thirteen heads in the breeze.

'Everyone! Gather round, stay together,' I say, counting heads and thinking about how I wasn't ready to get out of bed. I was... mmm, now is not the time!

'Okay, good, is that everyone?' I've counted, I know it's everyone but I ask all the same. It gives me a chance to turn my thoughts to the here and now. 'I want everyone to file through the turnstile. I have the tickets. When you get through, stop on the other side and wait for the rest, okay? Everyone got that?'

'Yes, Miss Clark,' they all chorus and on they go.

I'm glad to see the guide is already waiting on the other side. The kids are impatient and I don't want to have to deal with them. It would have been so lovely to stay at home this morning. I was... no don't think about it, now is not the time!

'Miss Clark?' the guide asks.

'Yes, that's me!' I say holding out my hand. She looks awfully young.

'I'm Sara,' she says, smiling, but she looks terrified and I wonder if she can handle this lot.

'Don't worry!' I tell her. 'They're nice kids, *very* enthusiastic, so the most important thing is for you to be loud and clear. Dominate their attention, don't let their thoughts wander.'

'Easy for you to say. You do this sort of thing every day. I just got this job,' she says and her face immediately goes red. 'Sorry, I didn't mean – I'm just new to all of this, I just–'

'–Trust me, you'll be fine,' I say, smiling with as much reassurance as I can muster, but my thoughts are slipping back to bed and my hands on his body; a smile, a kiss, a kiss, another kiss, each one harder and, *stop* it! This is not the time. I can feel myself flushing red. 'Okay, should we get started?' I say. I wind up my best teacher voice and let it go:

'Kids, gather round! This is Sara, and she'll be our guide today! Everyone, say hello.'

'Hello!'

'Sara's been working at the zoo for a *really* long time and she knows *loads* of interesting facts about all of the animals and habitats here, so if you have any questions, she's the person to ask. I want you to pay lots of attention to Sara because if you miss anything she says you might not get the *vital* answer to one of the test questions you'll be presented with back in class. I know you're all looking forward to the test!'

'Yes, Miss Clark,' they groan.

'Does everyone have their workpages ready?'

'Yes, Miss Clark,' they intone.

'Everyone have a stylus?'

'Yes, Miss Clark,' they drone.

'Well, let's get started then!' I say with my best smile. Sara gives me a stony look before grinning at the kids.

'Hi guys! It's great to meet you. Before we get started, can anyone tell me what they think of when they hear the word: *wildlife*? Come on, hands up, don't be shy!'

'Second Street on a Friday night,' Smart-Arse Steven calls out and everyone snickers. Uncertainty flickers over Sara's face before she gives him a broad smile and says:

'Yeah, me too! I think that's the real zoo.'

I'm a bit impressed. Smart-Arse Steven doesn't look like he knows how to respond. He shrugs and doesn't say anything. Sara drops the question. I think she knows what she's doing.

'Wildlife can mean a whole lot of things; it isn't confined to one perception. Today we're going to be looking at lots of different kinds of wildlife and some of it might not seem all that wild to you. I hope you'll be surprised by some of the things we consider wild. You won't find all of it interesting, but I guarantee you, *everyone* will find something they like in this zoo. If you can tell me honestly, at the end of the day, that there was nothing you liked, even a little bit, I will refund you your ticket. Mind, you have to convince me you're telling the truth, and I have an uncanny ability to smell lies!' she says, tapping a finger to her nose. The kids are hooked! 'So, we're starting in one of the most unassuming wildlife areas you may know of – the humble garden. Everyone, follow me!'

Sara walks down a path to the right of us. I catch up with her.

'Good work,' I say. 'I told you, you'd be fine.'

She frowns at me.

'You had no right to lie about me.'

'I was just making an introduction. They're more inclined to respect someone they think has a lot of authority. I was helping you.'

'You were lying,' she says and she turns to Good-Egg Greg and asks him a question.

I'm surprised by her hostility. I was only telling a little white lie. Most people would have found it funny. I think she's a little odd.

But she's not so odd. She's good. She knows when to make jokes and when to be serious, and she has an answer to everything. She knows this place. She could easily be everything I said she was.

'This is my favourite wild place,' Sara says as she brings us into the Island area of the zoo.

'Why?' asks Malcolm the Moron.

'Everyone gets a guess – let's see who's managed to suss me out. I'll give you two minutes to walk around, and look at the place before you guess. Then you can write your guesses down and send them to me.'

It's a nice move and gets them all fully engaged with the landscape. I want to say this to her, but she's determined to ignore me. I give up and take in the island myself. Perhaps I should make a guess too... God, it's been ages since I came to the zoo. It's more fun than I expected it to be. Maybe I should have tried to get Lewis here. No, he looked so sweet all wrapped up in my duvet. I... no, not now! But I do; I drift off on the sound of breakers and gull calls, and with the soft spray on my face and the smell of seaweed and salt in my nose. I drift off on it all and daydream, of us on a beach, touching each other, tasting each other, moving hard and fast against each other...

'Time's up, guys!' Sara's voice breaks in. 'Send your guesses to my tablet so I can look at them together.'

The kids line up and touch their tablets to hers – instant transfer – and she reads each one as she receives it, smiling over them all. I wonder what they wrote. I never smile at their work like that.

'Great work, guys! I'm really impressed by how deeply

you've thought about all the different aspects of this environment. And I'm pleased to say someone did guess why it's my favourite area. Isaac, you wrote: Because it's an island.'

'What! That isn't a real answer,' Piss-Me-Off Piper says.

'Actually, it is,' Sara says. 'This is my favourite environment precisely because it's an island. It's separated from other land masses by the sea, it's small and private, it's difficult to get to, it's exposed to the elements, it attracts wildlife you don't see anywhere else, it's empty and it has a stark beauty.'

'But those are all different guesses that everyone made!' Piss-Me-Off Piper says.

'Yes, but I can't just pick one of those guesses if all of them are true. Isaac's guess allowed me to pick everyone's guess, because everything about this island is what makes it my favourite wild place.'

'That's a load of turd,' says Smart-Arse Steven.

Sara looks at him and shrugs.

'In my opinion, Isaac made a clever guess. If you feel hard done by, feel free to complain to your teacher after the tour is completed. Now let's start breaking down–'

'–It's not really wild, though, is it? I mean you talk about each of these landscapes and animals as if we are really experiencing wildlife but none of it is true, is it? We aren't experiencing any life at all,' says Quiet Carly, which surprises me.

Sara looks at her and smiles, but I think she actually looks really sad.

'You ever heard of a snipe?' Sara asks her. Quiet Carly shakes her head. 'It's all lies. That's what people do: they lie. The best we can do is lie too – pretend and enjoy to pretend. So for today, let's pretend we really did leave a boring day behind to go on an adventure to all the wild places of the world. This is my favourite wild place and when I'm here it's easier to pretend I'm really somewhere else – somewhere out of the city – somewhere in the past. Unfortunately, we can never go to these places. Wildlife is behind us. But that doesn't mean we can't try to understand what it was like once upon a time.'

I'm absorbed in the speech. When I look at Sara again I notice she was crying as she said it. The kids don't seem to mind, though. They're just as absorbed as I am.

My vision is pulling out, pulling away, like one of those outer body experiences you read about when people talk about what it felt like when they died, like how I felt when I watched Jessie Wilkes die in that bog. I'm looking down on myself, only that isn't me. It's some woman. It's Miss Clark, the school teacher, who keeps thinking about her sex life. Even though I don't seem to have a body, I can feel myself shudder at her thoughts. Then my eyes (the ones I don't really have) focus on Sara. I remember the name and I remember the snipe and then everything seems to come back on me like vomit and suddenly I really am in my body and my skin is slick with sweat and I'm convulsing as my mind contracts and I feel as though everything should be coming out of me, being expelled, like waste. I feel my throat closing and I think perhaps I really am going to be sick, but of course there is nothing to come out. Thoughts don't fall out of your body. My mind is flypaper. Everything in the sim is sticking. And I'm not out yet, this ride isn't over. My stomach somersaults and I lurch through the air again.

'Arrrgggh!' I am afraid. I must run, but the... what is this stuff? It is on me, holding me tight, like a long snake wrapped around me. What is it all? I do not know and I cannot run! I hear noises, those creatures, the loud ones that know not the forest, and move like beasts not used to moving. They are coming to me, they did this to me! Why? I must run! 'Arrrrrgggh!'

'We have it!'

What are they saying? I do not understand, they speak with too much sound, and how frightening they are!

'It's a young one.'

'Smaller than I was hoping for, but look at him! Hairy little creature, isn't he! Hardly better than an ape.'

'Aaaarrrgh!' Keep away from me, creatures, keep away! How can I make them keep away? They grab me, their fingers pinch, they hurt. Let go of me! I struggle but there are more of them and bigger, stronger. I cannot escape. Let me go, let me go! What are they saying? I do not understand!

They are dragging me away, I struggle, I fight, I–

'He's a strong wee monster! Be careful, try and get a tighter grip on him.'

'He won't stay still, my – goddammit!'

'Keep a hold of him, for goodness sake!'

'I'm – trying. He's – stronger – than – I – expected!'

'Hit him! Hit – him – with – your – staff!'

'Ow! I – oof!'

Pain! I see black and my body is heavy. I try to find the light. I open my eyes. There is an evil smell, all around me. I do not understand! What is this place? What are these things around me? The ground I sit on is strange flat stones, all the same, one after the other. I have never seen stones like these. And ahead there is something brown and tall and flat and something about it is treeish but it is unlike any tree I have seen before. I try to move but I can't. There are snakes around me: cold, hard and noisy as I move.

I hear footsteps. I look for them. I see another treeish thing but flat and such a strange shape, like the stones, but bigger. The footsteps are behind it. It moves, swings towards me, and behind it is space, and filling the space is one of those creatures, the loud ones that move like beasts not used to moving, and it whistles and smiles and looks at me, and I am afraid.

It comes close, crouches down, reaches out and strokes my cheek.

'There you are, my beaut.'

I do not understand it. I hear footsteps and there is the other one, walking from the space beyond.

'Let's get him on the table, then!'

The creature in front of me, leans in, reaches behind and takes a hold of those cold snakes around me. It pulls the snakes, and me with them. I fall forwards but it does not hurt. I hear it laughing at me. It bends down and helps me up, but I find it difficult to stand. My legs tingle. It puts an arm around me and guides me to the treeish thing with the flat top. Then it forces me to sit down on the thing. Then it forces me to lie down on the thing. Then it makes the snakes around my wrists and ankles fast, and I am lying, and I am very afraid. I look, follow the creatures' movements, I struggle against the snakes, I–

'Fasten his head down, will you? He may struggle less.'

'Aaaaargggh!' They hold my head down, I cannot move it, 'aaaaaaarrrrrgggh!'

'Let's gag him. I won't be able to concentrate with that racket.'

They force something into my mouth! I want to spit it out, it tastes bad, evil, 'Aaaaarrrgggh!' I try to cry out, to find help, but my cries are quiet now; no one can hear me, help will not come. 'Aaaaarrrrgggh!' I cry again, a sad cry, a giving up cry. Then I cry no more. I struggle no more. I cannot get away.

'Good. That seems to have calmed him. Let's get started, shall we?'

I cannot see what they are doing. I cannot understand what they say. That bad smell, that evil smell, gets stronger. I feel cold on my stomach. I feel cold inside my stomach. A hand presses on my belly. And then there is pain – 'AAAAAARRRRRGGGGGGGGH!'

'Hold him steady, hold him steady!'

'AAAAAAAARRRRRRRGH! AAAAARRRRRGGGH! AAAAAAARRRRRRRGGGGHHHHH!'

Stop! I cry out, stop! But they cannot understand me. STOP!

I lurch.

'Are you ready?' asks a voice.

I feel fear. *No I don't.* The fear is subsiding, *what was I afraid of?*

'Yes,' I say and my voice is steady and cold. It's not mine, of course.

'Good man,' says the voice and she claps me on the shoulder. 'You're our star.'

'Are you sure about this?' asks another voice, a man.

'Of course he is,' says the woman. 'How many times do we have to go over this?'

'I just want to make sure! This is big, Sally. It isn't strikes and protests anymore. After we do this that's it. Everything will change.'

'That's the point! We're trying to make a difference. Things can't go on like this.'

'I *know* that, but so many people have already died.'

They're talking over me and I'm listening but I'm switched off, centred, focussed on the hard nut of resolve I feel in my stomach. I'm coiled up and ready. Besides, they've said all this before.

'–and what do you think is going to happen? We're facing the end as it is. We're in an extreme situation and it requires some extreme fucking action. Jesus, Greg. I don't know how many times we have to have the same argument. If you have to keep asking about this, you best start thinking about getting the fuck out because I'm not going to tolerate much more of this.'

'Tom's going to die!'

I look up at that.

'I know,' I say. 'That's how we'll get it done. And it's my choice. Not yours. So either get behind it or get out.'

Sally puts her hand on my shoulder again, grips it. I look up at her and she smiles. She doesn't look nearly so sure at that moment and I know it's because she loves me. She's a pearl.

'I'm ready,' I say, and I stand up. I feel strong, but the weight of everything is heavy on me. The weight of the bomb on my chest, the weight of the expectations. The weight of my hope. The weight of goodbye.

I take Sally's hand and give it a squeeze.

'This is the start of something. Don't back down.'

'Tom,' Greg starts, but I'm already walking away. I'm ready to die. I'm ready to kill a whole bunch of fat fucks too. I–

I've just been here, haven't I? The zoo. I'm sure I was here, only I... No, Miss Clark was here, and I was Miss Clark, and Miss Clark isn't real. I don't think. But we were here. Only the zoo looks different. And I feel different.

'Lottie!'

'I'm coming!' I say. *Lottie?* I'm moving towards the turnstiles and into the zoo and when I get inside I see it really is different. This isn't the kind of zoo I know. This isn't the kind of zoo Sara works in, it's much earlier than that. This zoo has real animals in it! I run up to Mum and Louise and I grab Louise's hand and we look at each other and laugh.

Mum rolls her eyes at us but she's smiling and she doesn't bother to ask us why we're laughing because she knows we're just laughing for the hell of it. Louise and I look at each other.

'Monkey House!' we say in unison, and we run flat out.

'Slow down, girls!' Mum calls after us.

'STOP!' shouts a man in front of us, but we're veering around him already, only he's pretty big and pretty fast and he shoots out a hand and grabs Louise by her arm and pulls us to a stop and it hurts!

'Hey!' Mum calls out and she heads for us pretty fast. Louise tries to squirm free from the man's grasp but he doesn't let her go.

'I told you to stop,' the man says. 'You shouldn't be running like that in the zoo. It excites the animals and not in a good way. You could seriously agitate them and–'

'Hey! Excuse me, but what gives you the right to go grabbing at my daughter like that? How dare you touch her!' Mum is furious and Louise and I trade a gloating smile. This guy is going to get it now. 'I could have you charged for that kind of behaviour I–'

'–I was just explaining to these young ladies here, that they can't run like that on zoo property. I rea–'

'–You have no right to go touching my girls, even if you are explaining zoo policy to them. A simple call would have sufficed, I–'

'–Excuse me, Madam, but I did ask them to stop, I–'

'–Ask them! You were yelling like a bloody mad man; it was terrifying. I don't suppose there's some sort of zoo policy about shouting is there? I'm sure shouting does the animals no end of good, does it? I think I'm going to have to–'

'–Madam, there was no way your girls were going to stop, I had to–'

'–I'm going to have to report you,' mum bulldozes over him. 'What's your name?' he squirms on the spot. 'Well? Spit it out!'

'Rick Markham.'

Mum gets out her legendary notebook and the red pen she likes to write everything in.

'Rrrick Maaarkham,' she says, drawing out his name as she writes it down. 'Now, that wasn't so difficult, was it?'

Rick Markham looks like he's ready to start running through the zoo now, just to get away from her.

'Now, Mr Markham. Have you anything to say to my daughters?'

Rick Markham looks venom at us and we can't help it, we're giggling.

'I'm sorry for grabbing you,' he says through gritted teeth. 'I hope you enjoy the rest of your visit at the zoo. Without running.'

Mum gives him a look that I know well. It's that triumphant look that Louise and I have perfected too. Rick Markham slips away, clearly relieved at escaping with his skin, and Louise and I start laughing really hard now. That's when mum rounds on us.

'I told you to slow down! That man had every right to stop you, in fact I think I should have just let him give you two a right old dressing down in front of everyone! You're lucky I'm not taking you home right this instant, but I promise you, when you get home you're going to make up for making me do that.'

Before I can stop myself I'm opening my mouth:

'Why didn't you just let him tell us off, then?' I ask and I can feel Louise squaring up beside me, ready to stand her ground too.

Mum narrows her eyes at us and holds our gaze and I'm regretting speaking. But she doesn't tell me off for talking back like I think she will. Instead she says:

'Only I have the right to tell my children off. Everyone else has to tolerate your bad manners. Though I thought I'd done a better job at training you to behave yourselves in public. Now that you've thoroughly embarrassed me, I think I'm going to have to do a lot more work on those manners. But since we're here already you may as well enjoy yourselves for a bit.'

Then Mum disengages.

'C'mon Lottie. Let's go,' Louise says, her tone subdued. I give Mum a tentative smile. She doesn't seem to notice and I see that she looks really tired. I suddenly feel a wave of worry for her. I'm about to reach out to her when Louise tugs at my hand. And just like that, the moment is broken. The monkey house beckons and off we trot.

The monkey house isn't just one house, really. It's lots of different enclosures, each fronted by a thick glass wall that lets us look into worlds that are supposed to be private. But I don't think that really, do I? I just love the zoo. Only I feel like there's someone in my head that thinks this is some kind of freak show we're seeing. Someone who hasn't seen this before. Someone who finds it all kind of sick. I shake my head and again, just like that, the moment is broken, the feeling of being invaded is gone.

'Look, Lottie!' Louise is pointing at the baby chimps.

Chimpanzees are her favourite and I have to agree that they are adorable. I watch them for a bit, the smallest one clutching to her mother's breast, her tiny hands, with their tiny fingers, just discernible from this distance. But I'm impatient to go and see Dora. Dora's an orang-utan. I'm not sure why I like her so much because when I think about it she's kind of ugly, but there's something special about her face. She sits close to the glass wall that separates us, and watches everyone pass through with this kind of intensity that makes me think she's memorising everything she sees. I go to take a closer look. She looks back at me. Her eyes are really gentle and all her movements are really slow and deliberate. And then, just like that, she stands up and comes over to where I'm standing, her wobbling walk making me smile. She's never done this before and I'm amazed. I don't move, I barely breathe. She sits right next to the glass in front of me and looks into my face, as if she's trying to burrow inside it and see what's in my head. Then her eyes move over me, tracing me; she's memorising those details. Very slowly, without breaking her gaze, she picks up some straw from the ground around her. She raises her arms and she puts the straw on her head. I'm confused by the gesture. A nearby child cries out:

'Look mummy! That monkey is copying that girl!'

I don't have to look at the kid to know he's talking about me and Dora, because now I see it. She's given herself blonde hair, just like mine. I smile at Dora and reach out a hand though I know I'm not supposed to touch the glass. And then I feel a strange sensation as if I'm falling inwards.

I see her. I have seen her. She likes to look at me. I wonder if she is like me. Or am I like her? But the thought is a silly one. I am not like them. I cannot be like them. I am a person of the forest. I long for the shadowy, green of the canopy. I miss my home, my mother, my trees.

There she is, looking at me. She wants to come inside, perhaps to live this life? This life behind a wall that I can see through, but not walk through. This life where everyone can watch me and I cannot have a moment in solitude. This life, unnatural and unwelcome. I did not choose this! Let me go! *LET ME GO!* She does not hear, does not see, she just smiles at me and puts her hand to the glass. I hold a hand up to hers – our hands meet but do not touch.

I long for the shadowy, green of the canopy, for my mother, who must be dead now, and my trees. I long for the forest.

'Go forth and sow your wild oats,' I say to the meagre assembly of students before me. 'Honestly. There's little point in any of you being here right now because our future doesn't require any more sociolinguists. At least, not imminently.'

What the hell is a sociolinguist? I wonder for a moment but of course I'm not me – I'm Thom Banks, Professor of Sociolinguistics at the College of New North Kingston, and I know all about this, I just need to take the time to acquaint myself with my own mind. In that time I have dual identity and in that doubleness I find it almost hysterically funny that I have just told a group of people that sociolinguistics doesn't matter. Because what I'm doing here, in this sim, is basically an exploration in sociolinguistics, isn't it?

'But...' I (Thom) continue, just as the first person begins to shuffle their papers indicating an inclination to take me seriously and depart, 'before you go, it would be remiss of me, as a sociolinguist, not to explain my choice of phrase. "Sow your wild oats." Hands up, those of you who've heard the phrase before.' It doesn't surprise me when everyone raises their hands. 'What does it mean?' This is that moment where all hands drop and everyone studies the table in front of them with remarkable intensity. But there's always one that keeps their head up. 'Yes?' I gesture to that one person, a girl in the front row (naturally).

'It's generally applied to men, and it means to go out and enjoy life, usually a bit recklessly. I guess it normally refers to sex. Like – "go and have sex with as many people as you can now, before you're attached to the ol' ball and chain".' She puts on a funny voice to say that last bit and I think to myself: Oh she's going to be lots of fun this semester, before I remember that there isn't going to be a semester.

'Great answer. For bonus points can you tell me why we use 'wild oats' in this phrase rather than say, domestic oats, or wild fennel, or... wild barley?'

She looks thoughtful.

'Well, I guess we use wild rather than domestic because we are talking about reckless behaviour, or impulsive rather than considered behaviour. But I have no idea why we use oats.'

I smile, because I like this phrase and in a way it seems more relevant now than it ever was; a comment on the big issues of today.

'I would have been pretty surprised if you had known. It's an answer that is unsurprisingly agricultural in nature, and if none of you have studied the history of agriculture, specifically oat farming, then you have no reason to know and no framework from which to guess. And the answer is both mundane and yet exciting. Well, it is if you're like me, and inordinately fascinated with the way society and language interact.

'*Avena Fatua,* also known as the common wild oat, is not actually an oat, but a weed. However, it's virtually impossible to tell it apart from our everyday oat grain and Avena Fatua likes to grow in the same places as our friendly, nourishing cereal. Before we had things like herbicides, farmers would have to inspect their crop, one plant at a time, and remove weeds by hand. Naturally, 'sowing wild oats' became a phrase to describe activities that were unprofitable. Oat grain also had a reputation for being a plant of 'invigorating' properties. A hop and a skip later, plant seeds are associated with human 'seed', and unsurprisingly the phrase becomes a reference to the sexual liaisons of free men, usually destructive ones. The liaisons that is, not the men. At least, not all of them. And these liaisons often resulted in the birth of bastards. Pretty negative stuff, huh?'

There is a general murmur of agreement, most of them actually look interested (but then this is an elective course), and I realise I don't have much more to say. After all, this isn't my specialty: cataloguing the history of phrases. This is just obscure knowledge.

'But when we use the phrase these days, it isn't so negative is it?' I continue with no idea where I'm going. 'It means go out and enjoy life! Take the bull by the horns! Yes have sex, yes be a bit reckless. It's a phrase we use to excuse bad behaviour, usually male. It's a phrase we use to encourage straight-laced squares to let go a bit. It's a phrase we use to explain why we feel comfortable doing things that used to be deemed inappropriate. It's a phrase we say to people when we want them to be free. Now that is pretty powerful positive energy. And all of this coming from a plant that adds no value to our lives whatsoever. The originating idea for the phrase has become incongruous with how we use the phrase today. So what changed? Well, we did, of course. We became more liberal, more forgiving in many respects, less ashamed of our proclivities and inclinations, our wants and desires. It follows that the phrase will die out eventually, redundant to a new society. A new phrase might take its place. However, and here is where I get really interested, if we look at the phrase and compare it with our current affairs, is it not just a perfect phrase to use in its older form? Is it not the very image of the negative changes that are taking place in our world right now? I mean if we get rid of the sexual element and just look at plants in general: nature is dangerous now. To sow wild oats... well, you reap a whole mess of troubles. In fact, we could give the phrase a dual purpose; when I say to you, 'go forth and sow your wild oats' I could be telling you to take the chance to be reckless now because pretty soon, due to the wild oats sown by society as a whole, we aren't going to have a chance to be so free. What do you reckon?'

I've run out of steam, been speaking without consideration, probably spouting utter crap, and I worry that I'll be judged by someone who's clever enough to pick holes in everything I've just said, but I also feel kind of thrilled at my audacity. Front-row-girl smiles at me and says:

'Well, it sounds like sociolinguistics still has a future, even if our future has no need for sociolinguists.'

Everyone laughs, and so do I.

'Sociolinguistics will always exist, so long as society and language interact. Don't study it now. Wait till it's necessary. Instead, go forth and sow your wild oats.'

I walk out. I'm done. I want to get on, go home, see my

wife, live a little, maybe sow a few wild oats of my own.

Zizania palustris oh! Oh! We like the feel of soft water at our roots. It laps and moves us in a languid dance. We sway in water and wind and we are wet. How cool and loving it feels. Oh! Yes, it strokes us, soothes us, pushes us, pulls us, and we drink it, how it fills us and makes us fat. We are heavy with water and we are heavy with grain, ripe, ready to yield. The water laps on wood. They part us softly, slap, slap, slap, their sticks in the water, and they glide and slide, closer, closer, and as they move, over the undulations they create, they stroke us with their... knockers they call them. They stroke us, brush us, gently, gently, releasing our fruits... oh! Oh! We drop our berries, our grains, our seeds, we drop our burden and we feel so light! As our bent backs straighten, as they ripple away, as we sway back into always, we hear them sing a song for the wild rice.

'Pull it tighter! Tighter! Oh come here!'

I hobble to her, the petticoat already feeling like it's cutting off the circulation in my waist. She's sitting on the bed, in the shadows, hiding from the morning sun that splashes through the big French doors. When I get to the edge of the bed her hands snake out into sunlight, her fingers take the drawstrings, and she pulls so hard I yelp.

'Hush now, it isn't that bad. You're making a fuss.' She deftly ties the strings off and fixes me with a critical look. 'You're too thin, my dear. We need to get some fat on these bones, neh?' She pinches the skin around my ribs. I wince but I don't say anything because she'll just tell me I'm fussing again.

'Okay, now fetch the sari, Gopi, chop chop. We don't have time to waste!'

I go to the big teak wardrobe and pull out the sari we

chose together. It's wrapped in tissue paper and plastic and for a moment I pause and just feel the weight of it in my hands. I unwrap it.

'Hurry up, girl, we don't have all day!'

This is so like Auntie. She says *I'm* making a fuss! I smile, though. I go back to her and she gets to her feet.

'Unfold it!' she commands.

I'm nervous to let it spill over the floor, I don't want to ruin it, but the material is long and there is nowhere for it to go but everywhere. Auntie doesn't take the sari from me but I can feel her impatience as I start to pull the fabric open. One fold, two fold, three and it touches the ground, and then there is nothing for it. I unfurl it quickly, listening to the crisp, tearing, noise as fabric that has been pressed together for years, is finally pulled apart, and I watch as the yellow silk puddles on the floor, melting into the sunlight until I feel as if Auntie and I are standing in a pool of honey. I gasp. Even though I've seen the sari before, it somehow seems more beautiful than ever, as though it's woven out of light. The thick red and gold borders keep the sari grounded and I feel as though the material would just vanish if those patterns weren't there. I rub the silk between my fingers and enjoy the soft, smooth, coolness of it. Suddenly I'm itching to get it on.

'Are you sure you don't want to put on a chiffon sari, Gopi? It's so hot, neh? Maybe a lighter sari will be better for you?'

'This is the one, Auntie,' I say and I look at her and from the way she's smiling I realise she wasn't being serious but making fun of my reaction to the sari.

'Okay, gulab jamun, it won't put itself on. Let's go, chop chop!' and Auntie bends down and, grunting, she picks up an end of the sari silk. 'Stand in front of me,' she says.

She tucks the end she has a hold of into the centre of the waistband of my petticoat. She just manages to pull the petticoat away from my waist, and before the silk fills the space I glimpse the imprint of the drawstring on my skin. Then she's tucking the edge of the silk around me, moving to my left, moving behind me and tucking, tucking, tucking. Then she's in front of me again:

'Are you paying attention, Gopi? I'm not always going to be putting your saris on for you, little madam. It's best you learn how, even if you don't wear them all the time.'

'Yes, Auntie.'

'Now here, you pleat the material, like so.' She folds the material back and forth, so well practised that I barely see what she's doing. 'See?'

'Yes, Auntie,' I say, knowing it's easier just to let her get on with it and to try on my own another day.

The pleats have created a thick wad of material which she somehow manages to squeeze into the petticoat, and I'm beginning to feel faint and uncomfortable.

'Auntie, I really think the petticoat is too tight.'

'Nonsense, Gopi. You don't want your sari falling off in front of everyone, do you? You just need to get used to it.'

I sigh and let her continue. She produces a nappy pin from thin air and pins the pleats through the petticoat to keep them in place. She takes the material around me once more and draws it diagonally over my body, laying it down over my left shoulder. Then she steps back, folds her hands over her belly and looks at me.

'Well?' I ask, nervous that she's going to say I don't suit it, that I should have chosen a different colour, a different material, or maybe even stuck to wearing an ordinary dress like I usually would. But she smiles. Auntie has an extraordinary smile. It's as if she has more teeth than anyone else and when she smiles you feel like you can count each one of them. You'd think it would be scary but it's actually the warmest smile I ever saw. Her teeth are strong and white (apart from the gold one that appeared one day without warning) and their brightness lights you up. It lights her up too; her eyes seem to sparkle as if they're catching the gleam of her teeth and mirroring it back. When she smiles I relax, instantly.

'Well child, you look just like your mother,' she says.

'Really?'

'Of course! Who else would you look like?'

I shake my head, thinking I could look like any of my relations. Then I step forward, kicking the silk a little so I don't trip on it, just the way I've been told to, and I make my way to the bathroom and the full length mirror. I haven't dressed my hair yet or put on my jewellery, but when I see myself in the sari thoughts of anything else are abandoned. Auntie is right. I look just like her. And I can't look at myself. I spin around and walk back into the bedroom.

'Gopi?' I hear Auntie ask, but I don't see her because I've crouched down on the ground and wrapped my arms around myself and I'm crying. 'Oh, Gopi,' Auntie says, and I feel her shadow fall over me as she walks between me and the French doors. She crouches down beside me, I can hear her knees clicking, and she puts her big arms around me and pulls me to her, pressing me into her round belly. I stop crying almost as soon as she touches me. I let her hold me for a moment. Then I pull back and wipe my eyes.

'Sorry, Auntie,' I say. 'I'm being silly.'

'No, gulab jamun. It's moments like this that we remember the loss, neh? Don't be afraid of your tears.'

I nod and, sniffing loudly, stand up and hold out a hand to help Auntie to her feet. She leans on me heavily as she rises. Then she walks back to the bed and sits down again.

'Ai! I am so creaky, child! Come. Sit down with me here. I'll plait your hair.'

I smooth down the silk of the sari before I go over to her. Then I sit down and turn my back to her. I feel her fingers thread through my hair, teasing out knots as they go, smoothing it out before she weaves it all together. We sit in silence for a while, and I just enjoy the feel of her playing with my hair. Then she speaks:

'This sari is made from tussar silk. My nanima brought it back with her after one of her trips to India. It was a special gift for Poonam. She was her favourite, you know? Poonam could do no wrong! My, that girl used to get up to all sorts of tricks, and if she was caught at something, you know she would blame it on me! Of course they always believed her; I was always getting into trouble for things Poonam did. But she was never mean. I've never met anyone with a warmer heart. Anyway, she was very proud of this sari when Nanima gave it to her. She wore it all the time; no one could get her out of it. Eventually, we persuaded her to give it a rest so as not to wear it out. She wrapped it up and put it away and after that, she only ever got it out for special occasions. When she wore it out to meet your father one night we knew it was serious! I mean, by then she barely ever wore saris. I can't remember the last time she wore this one but... oh, it made me smile when you picked it, out of all of them, to wear today.'

Auntie turns me around and strokes my cheek.

'You're her daughter through and through.' She fixes me with that brilliant smile of hers and I can't help but smile back. I feel a huge surge of love for her. In a way, Auntie is more my mother than the woman she's talking about. I hug her.

'Now how many times do I have to say this, Gopi? We haven't got all day! Let me finish your hair!'

I told her I was going for a walk.

'I'll go with you,' she said.

'I'm going for a real walk.'

She smiled at me quizzically, didn't understand what I was saying, and it pissed me off.

'*Outside*,' I said, and I could hear it in my voice, that 'you're so stupid' tone. And I wasn't sure if she deserved that. She isn't stupid. I mean it wasn't like she didn't get what I meant when I said outside. I didn't mean outside the apartment, or out on the street. I meant *this*. I mean will you look at it! This is it. Maybe I was just trying to shock her. Hell, I don't know what I was doing. I just knew I wanted to go for a real walk, and I knew I didn't want her to come, and I knew that she wouldn't want to come. Not *outside*.

'Oh' she said. I could tell she was upset. At the time I thought it was because I was coming out here. But right now, here, up on this hill, I think I know better. She was upset because I didn't want her to come. Don't get me wrong, she wouldn't have come no matter what, but that isn't the point. The point was that she wanted to feel for a moment that I wanted to share something with her. Even if I knew she'd say no, I should have asked. I think we both knew that I would have, if... but how I feel about her isn't the point. Hell, I don't know why I even said all of that.

Shit. I'll edit that bit out.

I'm recording this moment for how I feel about this – all of this – this landscape around me, this great outside. I want to share something with *you*, unnamed person watching this. I want someone, somewhere in the future, to know that there were still people like me around at this stage. People that were risking it. Going out. Trying to stay connected with it all. I want someone, somewhere in the future, to take inspiration from this. To maybe go outside themselves and risk it all. That's if you people in the future haven't already stopped hiding. You. You in the future: if you're still hiding inside then I'm not sure what hope we have. This is my attempt to inspire you.

So, here I am, turning the camera for a moment, so you can see my ruggedly handsome face. Hey there! This is me! My name is Cameron and I'm a little weird. Okay. I don't want to keep the camera on me; you get to see people like me all the time I reckon, so let's keep the lens on what you probably don't get to see. This! Isn't it amazing? I had to drive a good long while to get to this area. They've roofed most of the city now, you can still see it in the distance over there: the topless towers of New Victoria.

I drove. It's pretty difficult getting fuel but, if you have it, it's fairly easy to get out. No one really cares if you go out. They just aren't so keen on letting you back in. Processing for re-entry into the city can sometimes take days. I haven't been outside for ages, partly because of the trouble of re-entry, but also because of my family. I don't want to go into it; that's not why I'm doing this; I'll just say that shit got complicated and then I met her and shit got more complicated. For a while I forgot what it was I really loved. But not today. Today is all about the truth. And I believe that the truth of the matter is this: we should be out here!

So. Let me show you around.

If you look carefully, you'll notice signs, almost everywhere, of our previous habitation out here. It astonishes me how quickly nature took hold after we retreated, but it can't erase us completely. We are indelible. I think that is a pretty negative thing, but in a way I'm kind of proud of how fucking stubborn we are. I just wish we had used that power in a good way. Anyway, this isn't about us, this is about all of this *outside*. This is my favourite area to come out to. I like it here because of the height. The higher you go the clearer the air feels and tastes. I feel like I'm bathing in clean air up here. And it gives the best view. I mean, look at all of this! You can see everything: the network of living space we used to occupy, the gardens, woods, parkland; there's a lake over there, and on a clear day you can even see the sea in the distance. And, contrary as it may sound, I love looking at the city from here.

There is one other thing I like about this area. You may have noticed that I have steadily been walking us away from our starting point, and that's because I want to show you this other thing up close and personal. Okay, hang on a minute. Let me figure out the zoom on this thing. I just bought it and I haven't quite worked it all out. Okay! Right, let's get right in there. There it is! Beautiful isn't it? Nah, I'm kidding. I can't imagine you know what the fuck I'm doing, so let me just explain it to you. This little shrub that I am focusing on is called *Thymus serpyllum*. I doubt you'll recognise it. To be honest, I didn't know what it was the first time I saw it, and I didn't care all that much until I saw... wait for it... I was hoping I would say 'until' and then miraculously, as if on cue, one of them would appear but no such luck... let's wait for a bit. Just keep staring at the thyme... there! Oh God, focus, hang on a minute, let me just get the focus right and... there! You see it! A honey bee! I couldn't believe it the first time I saw one. I just sat here for ages, watching. And there wasn't just one.

Look! Look over there! See, there are quite a lot of them out here, actually. They seem to stick to the thyme flowers – which is why I know this little shrub is called thymus serpyllum; I looked it up when I got home. Later, I found their hive, but I was scared of somehow... I dunno, I was scared I might kill them without meaning to or something. So I kept my distance and usually I just watch them from here.

They give me hope, you know. That it isn't all lost. Things can go back to how they were, maybe. We just have to not be scared of it. I mean, would you look at them! We thought they were all gone.

Let's just watch them for a bit. Watch them, people of the future! If you're still hiding inside, watch them right now and think – they came back from the brink! Why can't it all come back? Why can't we all come out and put it all back together?

'Bang! Bang, bang, bang!'

What the hell is going on? I know exactly what this body feels like and I'm really scared now. I mean I've been plenty scared this whole time but now I'm terrified because this isn't just some person I'm slipping into, some person I don't know and yet know, some person I am and am not, someone I can decipher later and think over, separately, divorce myself from; this person I've just slipped into is me! But not *me* me; this is old me. And by old me I don't mean *old* me, I mean me from before. I mean young me. And maybe you think: what's so scary about that? You're yourself finally, right? What's terrifying me is this one question I have: how does the machine know? I mean, this sim is plugged into my wrugs. The computer is communicating with nerve endings in my wrists making the experiences I'm having feel real. It has no access to my mind, my thoughts, my memory. So how is my memory a simulated experience? Is it just a freak incident? Is my memory accessible for everyone or does everyone experience a simulation that involves themselves?

The questions, the fears, they flicker through me too quickly for me to really read them, though because I'm being carried away by the tidal wave of sim and I'm young me and I'm shouting:

'Bang! Bang, bang, bang! You're dead!'

I watch as Cliff slowly turns around. I've been looking forward to showing him the wooden pistols and the holster Mum gave me at the weekend. She told me they were hers when she was a girl and she had loved to play cowboys and indians with her sister. When she showed them to me I thought I hadn't seen anything so wild. I thought me and Cliff could play with them at break time. But as soon as I see his face I know I made a big mistake.

'What are those?' he asks me and I can hear the sneer in his voice.

'They're guns,' I say but I've lost heart and my voice is really quiet.

'What?'

'Guns,' I say, much louder. And I know I've made a terrible mistake even thinking that Cliff would be interested. Cliff is one of the wild kids. He is *the* wild kid. He doesn't have time for tameos like me. And what's more tame than a set of guns? How stupid!

'Guns,' he echoes and I can hear him gearing up for a bout of ridicule. He snatches up the gun in my hand then.

'Wood! A wooden gun! Hey everyone!' He shouts and just like that, because he's Cliff, everyone comes over.

'Look at these!' He throws the gun he's holding to Will who snatches it out of the air.

'What's this supposed to be?' Will asks and I can hear how stupid he is in his voice, but people still like him because his mum always gives him the newest tech before anyone else because she works as a software developer for *Sixthsense*.

A flicker of annoyance crosses Cliff's face and I can tell he finds Will's wits, or lack thereof, tedious, but that he feels like he has to put up with him because he's Will.

'It's a gun,' Cliff says, going over to Will and snatching it back. 'Wooden guns to play with!'

Everyone laughs now and I feel all eyes on me. My mouth goes dry and my heart beats faster. It isn't that I'm afraid exactly; it's that I feel hurt. Last year me and Cliff did everything together. He lived with his dad in the apartment next door and when we weren't at school together we were in each other's homes. My dad always said we were conjoined. Cliff has a good imagination and he can make a game out of anything. I think last year he would have loved these guns. But I should have known better than to try and approach him now. I was too unpopular and my wooden guns were too tech basic.

Anyway, my stomach clenches into that twist like the water is being squeezed out of it and that's when I have one of my moments where I go somewhere else. Dad says it's my coping mechanism. I check out. Only I don't really check out. It's more like I separate my thoughts from what's happening to me. So I see everyone laughing at me and pointing. Cliff's waving the gun over his head and pretending to shoot me. He's doing it with that kind of exaggerated movement that shows he's mocking me and I can hear his voice but only as if it's coming at me from a distance:

'Bang bang bang! Die! Die!'

And that's when Will muscles in. He pushes me.

'Die!' he says. 'Die!' and he pushes me harder.

Someone comes in from behind and pushes me from the back and they are pushing me between them now, back and forth. 'Die,' they echo, 'die!' And it becomes a chorus and the whole playground is ringing with 'Die! Die!' and there's Cliff 'bang bang bang! I shoot you down!' The pushes get harder, and now I'm ringed around and I can feel hands pummelling at my back and on my chest. They catch me, hard, and give a little before throwing me, hard, ahead, and I bounce – boing boing boing – between everyone and I think it probably hurts as they all throw me around and chant 'die, die, die' but I don't notice, not really, because I've checked out and I'm watching from a distance and all I can think is: isn't it funny how I boing, boing boing? It's really funny. So I laugh out loud. And once I start laughing I can't stop and the laughs ripple through me so I feel like I have hands pushing me from the inside as well as the outside and the idea makes me laugh even harder until I feel tears coming out of the corners of my eyes and it's only then that I realise I've stopped boinging back and forth and that they aren't shouting 'die' and 'bang' at me anymore. The only sound in the playground is me laughing.

'What a freak,' I hear Will say.

Everyone titters nervously. I see Cliff drop the gun.

'C'mon. Let's get out of here,' he says. 'We've got better things to do.'

Just like that, everyone is gone and I'm still giggling as I lean forwards and pick up the gun and stick it into the empty holster on my hip. I'm giggling but I don't feel like things are so funny anymore, and I feel the consequences of all that pushing on my torso, and the more I come back to myself the less good everything seems until I'm fully there, standing in the middle of the playground on my own, and I want to cry because the humiliation is just hitting me.

That's when I hear her. Kel.

'I like your guns,' she says.

I look at her and I'm suspicious. I've known Kel for ages but we don't talk. I don't think I've ever seen her be mean, but after what just happened I'm feeling really untrusting of everyone. Because Cliff used to be my best friend. How can someone go from being your best friend to being... that? What he just was.

'Yeah,' I say.

'No, I'm serious,' Kel says. 'I like them. Can I take a closer look?' and she holds out a hand and she looks at me with a weird soft expression, like she's expecting me to run, but she wants to stop me if she can.

I nod at her because, in spite of everything, I'm still pretty proud of these pistols. I hold one out to her and she takes it and turns it over in her hands, inspecting all the lines.

'It's great!' she says. 'But how d'you play with them?'

'Mum says she used to play cowboys and indians with her sister.'

'What's cowboys and indians?'

'Mum says it's like a fighting game, kind of. You have two sides, the cowboys and the indians. And they fight with each other.'

'Why do they fight with each other?'

I shrug.

'Because they're afraid of each other, I think. Dad said he was going to show me an old vid of something called a western. He said there were lots of cowboys and indians in it.'

Kel nods and gives me the gun back.

'I really like them. Maybe when you see that vid you can tell me more about how to play?'

'Why don't you come home and watch it with us?' I say.

'You serious?'

'Yeah.'

'I'll have to ask Mum or Dad. I'm not sure.'

'Well let me know,' I say. The bell rings. 'C'mon. Let's go to class.'

There's a slipping sensation and I find myself sitting at home on the sofa next to Dad. There's a vid projecting from the computer in front of us.

A land stretches out before us, barren and brown, small scrubby shrubs sprouting here and there like a weird kind of acne. The land is flat and open and we can see for miles. There's a dust-cloud directly ahead of us and it's getting bigger. Dimly, I hear cries, chants of war. I'm tense with excitement. Then they break through the cloud and I can see them: the red men! Dad says we can't call them red men now but that people used to call them that a really long time ago because they didn't realise that they were really just regular people. They called them red men because they didn't understand them.

The red men whoop and chant and I'm mesmerised because they're unlike anything I've ever seen before. I mean they're people like other people (and I know plenty that look like them), but they're also entirely different. For a start, they're on horses. Horses! I never knew horses were this big. And the men – there are only men – are beautiful, their skin rich, dark and gleaming in the sunlight. They wear leather trousers and soft soled shoes and their chests are bare, covered in bright paint in the shape of hands and hieroglyphs. Many of them have long dark hair, sometimes loose, sometimes braided, and many of them have bright feathers braided in their locks. One man, at the head of the charge, is wearing a huge head-dress, all beads and feathers and leather. It reaches up to the sky and swoops down over each of his shoulders and I wonder how he can support it on his head as he gallops towards me. I whisper the question to my dad, even though talking brings me out of the moment. I have to know!

He smiles and tells me it's an historical inaccuracy. Headdresses like that would've only been used for special occasions in Native American camps – they're Native Americans, not red men or Indians! – maybe for festivals or shamanic rituals. I'm about to ask him what shamanic rituals are when the red men – the Native Americans – get right up to us, maybe a hundred metres away at most:

'WooWooWooWoo' they cry, hitting their mouths with the flats of their hands, making the sound warble into the sky. And the earth around us explodes as, from the unseen areas of the flanks of the sofa, cowboys charge out. I see the bouncing backsides of their horses as they fly forwards, and I see their backs. The cowboys are a lot less impressive than the Indians. The Native Americans. Even though they're on horses too, they're too familiar. They're fully dressed for a start, and their clothes don't seem a whole lot different from what people wear nowadays. Some of them are even wearing jeans! How old are jeans?! They're wearing pretty wild hats, though. I ask Dad if this is pretty much true. Dad says that all the really old westerns weren't very accurate. He says that history's pretty funny. It belongs to the people that record it and we're only ever given the history people want us to have. He also says the further away things happened the less we care about them. The history everyone looks at is the stuff that made everything the way it is now. I tell Dad that even if it's all a lie, those red men are wild.

It's only later on in the vid that I'm really impressed by the 'cowboy' character. I'm basically in the spot of the hero of the story so I can't see him, it's like he's standing right behind me. His name is Wild Bill. Anyway, he stands behind me and the villain, a nasty cowboy that's murdered a lot of people and terrorised the town and the Indians around it, stands opposite me. He's chewing tobacco. He spits out a hunk of it and some of the spit dribbles out in a red string that attaches itself to the skin of his chin. It's pretty disgusting. I guess he looks horrible to show how mean he is inside. He stands there and leers at me and Wild Bill behind me.

'You gon' shoot me now, boy?' he asks.

I hear Wild Bill shift his feet behind me, his spurs jingling.

'Yep.'

'You think you're fast enough?'

I see Wild Bill's shadow nod.

The bad guy laughs.

'Okay,' he says.

There's a long pause. The moment seems to stretch. Everyone in the town is either lining the streets or peeking out of windows. There isn't a sound other than the buzzing heat of the noonday sun. And then it happens so fast I don't even realise it's happened at first. I see Wild Bill's shadow move, his gun pointing out ahead of him and I see the surprise spread over the villain's face. Then I hear the bang. The villain looks like he's about to say something. He falls to his knees instead. Then maybe he's going to say something, now. But, instead, he falls to his side. The vid vision swoops up so I'm hovering above him now, like I'm the sky. He's looking up at me, but his eyes aren't focussed. Blood is spreading out on the dirt beneath him. His skin grows pale as I watch him. I notice that the tobacco spit isn't on his chin anymore. The lack of consistency reminds me I'm not watching something real, and I let out my breath which I didn't know I'd been holding. I look at Dad and he smiles at me. And then the place is filled with the happy cries of the liberated town, and I'm thinking: that Wild Bill was fast! How wild!

But even though I like the cowboys now (well, some of them) I think if I play cowboys and indians with Kel I'm going to have to be an Indian! I wish she could've come over and seen it. But maybe it's good she didn't because she might've wanted to be an Indian too and we can't play indians and indians. Maybe we could take turns, though.

'Dad, can we get a bow and arrow like the ones the Indians use? And can we make a headdress with all those feathers?'

My mind is full of the west: cowboys, Indians, the land and the horses and everything that's both strange and different and yet familiar and the same.

~~I went for a wander in the woods one day...~~

No, that's rubbish. How about –

~~I was wandering the wildwood...~~

Terrible!

~~Where the wildwood winds...~~

Woods don't wind though do they?

Where the wildwood... The wildwood, the wildwood, the wildwood...

I'm going to be tapping this pen all day, aren't I? Maybe I should go for a walk. I need a walk in the woods, really, don't I?

Okay. Take five hundred.

Once there was a wood. A wild one. And there was no one there to see it.

The trees spoke to each other, in creaks and moans, voices susurrant and when the wind blew they danced, crowns caressing each other in a show of affection. When the wind blew they laughed.

First came the conifers, hardy and hard. There was a spikiness about them that should make one wary. There was the odd birch, its trunk all eyes, the watcher of the wood, and a few aspens, slender and shy. Sycamores, strong, their branches spreading, and alders also.

The weather warmed.

The conifers retreated from the heat. Cold hearts require cold climes.

Strangers took their places. Yews, fat and friendly, crowns in disarray, crooked crookéd branches beckoning. Junipers emerged. And then, with a flurry of fallen leaves, the 'decidueds' flourished. Poplar, rowan, beautiful beeches, lime, elm, holly. The mighty oak! Hawthorn, ash, maple, willow, hornbeam, hazel, cherry and oh! the delightful crab-apple. Imagine this arboreal world.

The trees were all. Shelter, shade, home, hideout, they nurtured and nourished; even as they died they gave life. The trees were all. Once there was a wood. A wild one.

And there was no one there to see it, but the trees themselves and the creatures that called them home.

Once there was a wood.
And then someone saw it.
And the wood was no more.

8

Hence ~'ISH1 *2 a.*, ~'LY2 *adv.*, ~'NESS *n.*

There was a flash of light – white, blinding – and a piercing pain in my head. Eeeee! A screech, like microphone feedback, but coming from inside my ears. Another flash of light and I saw myself. I was sitting at a computer in the word museum, wrugs jacked, face pointed at the computer screen. What the... the image flickered, disappeared into blackness, then blinked back in front of me. Me – computer. The perspective shifted and I lurched into myself, peered through my own eyes, saw the screen in front of me and on it were the words:

Hence wildish wildly wildness **ERROR**

I heard the stutter of software malfunctioning. My stomach dropped, that falling sensation when panic is just about to take over. I looked at the screen and thought that **ERROR** actually said **TERROR** and I remember thinking for a split second: how appropriate! Before the white light shot through my eyes again and, with a sudden crescendo, the screeching screeched out of existence and I was left in a dark place, with the sensation that I was breathing and sweating heavily, though I couldn't know if any of those feelings were real.

9

adv. In wild manner (*shooting wild*).

And the next thing I knew was that the darkness had lifted because I'd opened my eyes, but I was still breathing and sweating heavily... and I'm not myself. I'm there, in the background, but I'm more someone else. A soldier, a spotter, and I'm looking through my scope, eye trained on the doorway of a building. I'm afraid. Fear twists my guts and I can taste it, metallic, in my mouth. But the fear is thrilling too. I'm willing the target to appear.

I take my eyes away from the scope for a moment, glance at the sniper next to me, but I don't say anything. I look back through my scope and wait.

The heat is oppressive. I can feel sweat gathering on my scalp, trapped into place by my hair. Occasionally a drop drips down my forehead, down into my face, a salty skin tear, it tickles, tries to distract. Flies follow the tracks left on my skin. They settle on my face, probing at the flavour of it with whatever that sucker they use to taste things is called. The tickling of their feet can be ignored. The general discomfort is endurable. This is what I was trained for. I wait and watch, stomach pressed to the ground, eyes trained, and the sweat pools and drips, the flies tickle and buzz, and the day gives way to darkness.

My partner and I take shifts in watching. We don't talk. There's nothing to say and the quiet is safe.

Light grows. It isn't long before the heat sets in. The temperature should be nothing to me. But it's hot. I watch. He watches. We keep the silence. Sweat pools and drips, flies tickle and buzz. Nothing else moves but the haze of the heat and the occasional drift of sand in the wind. The building is dead. Sweat pools and drips, flies tickle and buzz, and day gives way to darkness.

My partner and I take shifts in watching. We don't talk. There's nothing to say and the quiet is safe.

I try to find it: that moment when darkness gives way to day but it's so slight it's impossible to pinpoint. I don't find it, even approximately. And when I notice what I'm doing I realise my mind isn't where it should be. It should be out there, watching. So I shift focus. Scan harder. Nothing seems to have changed. I pray nothing changed. My partner doesn't speak. The light grows. The heat grows. I watch. He watches. We keep the silence. Sweat pools and drips, flies tickle and buzz. Nothing else moves but the haze of the heat and the occasional drift of sand in the wind. The building is dead. Sweat pools and drips, flies tickle and buzz, and day gives way to darkness.

My partner and I take shifts in watching. We don't talk. There's nothing to say and the quiet is safe.

What strikes me most about this place is sound. There's none but the flies buzzing and they don't buzz much at night. At least silence is how it seems at first. But there's a beat I can hear, a pulse. I can't tell if it's my own or if this place is breathing somehow. And there's the occasional sound I can't identify. A hollow cry, not an animal, maybe wind, funnelling through corridors walled by sand. Is it an exhalation? Once I heard an animal in the night. It made a sort of kek-kek-kekking sound. I don't know what it was.

Day breaks. Heat breaks. I watch. He watches. We keep the silence. Sweat pools and drips, flies tickle and buzz. Sweat pools and drips, flies tickle and buzz, and nothing moves but the light as day gives way to darkness.

My partner and I take shifts in watching. We don't talk. There's nothing to say and the quiet is safe.

The darkness gives way to day. I watch. He watches. I watch. He watches. I watch. He watches. I watch. He watches. I wat–

I stiffen and with a voice that barely breathes I say:

'It's time.'

The building isn't dead. It comes alive with people like some magic trick, and my eyes are full with movement, and my ears are full with sound as men and women call to each other: talking, joking, someone is singing, and my eyes are searching searching searching for the one.

We have our target. One man. One shot, one kill. He's in our sights. We don't talk. Everything has been said. We know the distance. We've read the wind, we've calculated all the angles, we know heat and humidity. My partner knows what he's doing, he's got a gift, he just has to take the shot, and we can get the hell out of here. I keep my eye to the scope, he pulls the trigger, I watch the shot, I see the vapour trail distorting the air, drawing my eye, I watch it travel, I see it hit, I'm ready to pack up and run, escape route unfolding in my head as I pull back, but my eye is drawn, I stay at the scope, another vapour trail... and another...

I pull back and look at the sniper. He's intent, loading and reloading. I want to say something but I've forgotten my voice. I move instead, try to take the rifle from him. Oddly, he gives it up easily. I think he's done, it's time, we can go. And then sound explodes – RATATATATATATATATATATATATATATATATAT – and it's not coming from them.

He has my rifle; the one I never used, the one I kept beside me just in case, and he's shooting at everything. I don't need my scope to see the soldiers, people, all falling down, he's killing them all and I don't know what to do so I just grab what I can and run. I run! I'm afraid. Fear twists my guts and I can taste it, metallic, in my mouth. But the fear is thrilling too. I was willing the target to appear. I was willing any target to appear. I wanted this, what he did. I wanted to shoot. Shaking the thrill from me, I run.

10

n. desert, wild tract; (out) in the ~ s, (colloq.) far from towns etc. [OE *wilde* = OS, OHG *wildi*, ON *villr*, Goth. *wiltheis*, f. Gmc * *wilthijaz*]

I run. As I run I feel myself falling away and being replaced by someone else. I'm not real and this someone else is. Wait... am I not real? I – I feel myself flooding into this soldier, filling her body as it runs into the desert, only her body isn't hers anymore.

I'm running. Running into the desert. And this desert is alive, I can hear it breathing. The sand is fine, a baked buff colour, and it slips under my feet. I'm running down a corridor, dunes rearing up on either side of me like bleached waves, and in front of me, rushing into me, is a wind that throws up eerie sound. The sound of the desert. I'm running and for a moment I have a perfect awareness of everything: How small I am, how alone, how immense this desolation is, the heat of the sun, the inconstancy of the sand beneath my feet, the danger I'm in, the yawning quiet... I'm running and the desert keeps stretching out, endless. I run and I feel this strange elation because I'm myself and I'm alone. I push my body harder, run faster, and I think: *I'm running out of existence now!* And it's so sweet that I can't bear to slow down, I can't bear to be anywhere else, I can't–

One moment I'm running through desert, and the next the whole world has changed, though I'm still running, so help me! I spring up from soft sand and I land on hard red soil, sparsely clad in tough, wiry grass. I cover a few metres, driven forward by my momentum, but then I come to a stop. Time to inspect another hell, just for me.

I notice the sounds first. After the eerie wailing, and the stretching quiet of the desert, it feels as though my ears are being assaulted. The air is thick with the clicks, whirrs, buzzes and scratches of a rich insect life. How do I know that? I'm through asking questions. I pick through the other sounds.

'Qoohoo, Qoohoo' a bird calls.

'HAdeDa! HAdeDa!' says another. And this is just the beginning, I can't isolate everything, I can't even hear everything, there's so much going on.

I look around, absorbing details. I see the red earth give way to a sea of grass, long and undulating, green and gold, a savannah-scape. Breaking the grassland here and there are small shrubs and sharp, thin trees. On the horizon, hazy and grey with distance, the ground rises into hills. Just ahead of me, something moves. It has a big body. Not enormous, but big. It's the colour of a shadow and the only reason I see it at all is because it moves. And it isn't alone. The whole world is walking with it. There are hundreds of them, and they're strange. They remind me of cows (I've seen pictures), but they're also totally different. They have longer, thinner legs. Their necks are thick and covered with strips of long black hair; a patchy, punk rock kind of mane. Their noses curve forwards, making them look sort of dignified despite the absurdity of the way they've been put together. They have small horns. I watch them and imagine their eyes: doleful, as though aware of their idiotic aspect. Their backsides are too small, their shoulders are too big, and they have long swishing tails. Beast after beast walks before me; they've taken over the whole landscape, and as I watch them, fascinated, their name drifts into my thoughts: wildebeest.

I'm staggered by the sheer number of them. I sit down and try to count them as they pass. The sun is hot overhead but a cool breeze drifts over me. I hear the grass rustling, and the hum of life that seemed so violent, so loud at first, has dissolved into a pleasant background music. There's a wonderful smell, something I've never known before, and though it's strange, I know it. Earth, growth, life.

It's funny to think that nature is now unnatural. Funny that language hasn't evolved to accommodate the change. Not fully. Not yet.

My eyes grow heavy. I fight the urge to sleep, but as I sit and listen to the wildebeest grunt and low, I go blank. It takes time for me to realise that the gentle 'Ummoo's' of the animals have been replaced by more urgent, guttural calls. I hear the hard clap of hooves as the wildebeest scatter in different directions, galloping. They become a mass of darkness churning in front of me. As I watch this whirlpool spinning into existence it doesn't occur to me that maybe I should move. I'm enthralled. I can sense fear but I can't see what they're afraid of. So I just keep watching, following one, then another, then another, and then a gap opens up between one wildebeest and all the rest and as this enormous, incongruous, creature dives forward I see something move in its wake.

I've never seen a cat like this, but I know it. It's bigger than I imagined, and far more beautiful. Its thick fur is a sunset of oranges and yellows and black rosettes blossom over it. It moves with deadly grace.

The cat dives after the wildebeest and as the beast veers left the cat anticipates it – a perfect hunter – it's there already, rising up and leaping forward. It embraces the beast, forelegs wrapping around its neck, its mouth going in for a kiss, and I wonder: *why is the wildebeest struggling?*

The wildebeest fights, pulls back with all its strength, and all the while the cat seems calm, to hold the beast firm, running forwards with it as it backs away, totally at ease. It moves like liquid. It stops as the wildebeest stops. And suddenly it's pushed backwards, the wildebeest drives it back, shakes it, moves it, this way, then that. And the wildebeest jerks back, it finds space, a moment of uncertainty where anything can happen, and the cat has lost its grip. I expect the wildebeest to turn and run, kick out one final time and flee, but it's braver than that. It stands there, head bent, and I can tell it's getting ready to charge and I turn to the cat. I can feel my throat tensing as if I'm getting ready to shout.

But I don't shout.

The wildebeest rushes forward. The cat backs away, still looking for a chance to gain purchase on her prey, and I don't know why I've decided she's a she, or why I'm on her side, but I'm on her side and my heart hammers as I watch that wildebeest charge, controlling the path the cat takes, head bent, horns looking mighty sharp. Those horns seem to take up the whole land-space and I can't help myself – I cry out. I cry out as she screams and out come the horns, slick with blood. The wildebeest spins and runs as though it would take off and fly. I watch it escape and part of me is glad and part of me is sad and I wish for a moment that every possible outcome of this could happen, that every wish could be fulfilled, that both cat and wildebeest could get what they wanted, what they needed, what was right, and I wish right then that I could be anywhere but where I was.

But the sim isn't finished with me. I watch the wildebeest race away like a cloud shadow across the grass. Under the clatter of their hoofbeats and the grunts of their efforts and their fear, I can hear the cat keen. I can't see her in the long grass, but I want to do something for her. I want to help.

So I stand up and walk to where I saw her fall, where I can hear her crying. I walk slowly and although I'm sure of what I'm doing, I'm nervous. I remember Ms Sneddon saying once that animals had better senses than we did. I think: *if I'm afraid she'll know*. So I stop and stand still until I feel calmer.

When I'm ready, I move, keeping my steps quiet and slow. She isn't crying anymore but I can see where she is, ahead, where the grass is lying different. As I get closer I make myself smaller. I crouch, and I'm not sure why but I know that this is so she won't be threatened by me. I slow down again. I know she's listening to me. I inch through the grass. And then I see it: one more curtain of long grass; if I pull it aside, there she'll be, lying down, nursing her wounds, probably licking at the blood.

I kneel and reach forward both hands to separate the grass. Not a tremor to them. My hands that is. The grass bends easy, thick as it is, and I can see her flank just there, rising and falling as she breathes heavy, the fur thick and lustrous, begging me to touch it. I don't. I look up and see her face is turned towards me. Her eyes meet mine, the dark pupils so big I start to wander into them, and I feel like I know what she's thinking. I feel that she's scared of me but that she knows I'm not there to hurt her and as I look at her, I'm falling in love, and that's when I reach out. I reach for her face, and she doesn't even take a moment to think about it. She's on her feet and she leaps at me.

I can't quite register what's happening; my brain is only half recording the facts because the panic that's flooding my body makes it impossible for me to really understand anything. I feel the heat of urine, but I'm more concerned with breathing. I can't breathe. She hit me in the chest, landed on me, and her weight is squeezing my lungs. I try to move, feel my hands scrabbling at the earth and grass, trying to gain a purchase on something to help me move, something to make her move and she's snarling into my face and I can smell the rot of meat on her breath. I can feel the heat of her, and blood is dripping into my face from the wound in her chest, but that wound isn't anything, really; this girl is alive! And she's suffocating me. My head hurts. All I can see is her face, her eyes gold and green, the pupils narrowed down to a shaved lemon slice of darkness, but even as I look at her, her face is getting darker, my vision blurring, my breath isn't there anymore and I want her to kill me quick because this is unbearable. I catch a glimmer of her teeth, but only a glimmer. I can't see more, and I hope she's opening up that jaw to take a bite, to give me that, just give me that, please give me that one thing, I wish I wish I wish and I–

BREATHE!
BREATHE!
BREATHE!

I breathe! The rush of air through my mouth, down into my lungs, is divine. And it hurts! It hurts so much! Because the air burns my throat, and my chest can't expand to take it all in, there's too much pain. I'm broken in, crushed, and I try to scream, try to call for help but I can't make a sound, I can only breathe, but I know that I'm alive. I know I'll be alive for a little while longer. So I breathe.

11

adj. slang. Anything or anyone deemed to be very good, interesting, fun, exciting etc. Positive description.

'Breathe' I tell myself, 'breathe'. I don't say it out loud because I can't breathe enough to talk, and the only reason I'm saying it at all is so I've got something to focus on, so I don't panic so much I actually stop breathing. After a time I find I'm getting used to the pain in my chest, I'm getting used to not getting enough air. I'm not scared anymore either. I blink open my eyes. I'm lying flat on my back which seems normal to me given I can't breathe and my chest feels like a cracked egg. I'm looking up at a white ceiling but it isn't just white. There are these small twisty black things creeping all over it and I can't work out what they are. They're blurry, out of focus, but there's something familiar about them. They march across the ceiling with regularity, as though they're moving on an invisible conveyor belt, out of the room and back into the room, over and over again. I'm assuming I'm in a room. I watch the twisty black things, blur across the white, try to focus on them now, and I can't work out if their blurriness is due to the pain I'm in or the distance they are from me. But the fact that I'm trying to work things out seems like a good sign, and as the questions surface the blurriness seems to subside. I can see them more clearly now: words. Of course! Words, that read:

> 11. *adj. slang.* Anything or anyone deemed to be very good, interesting, fun, exciting etc. Positive description. **ERROR ERROR ERROR ERROR TERROR ERROR TERROR**

And it HURTS!

I can't really say much about what happened immediately after that. See, I was totally gone for a few days. But this is what I pieced together later on, from everyone else. Apparently, I had some kind of seizure – a reaction from prolonged exposure to rigorous stimuli. One of the staffers at the word museum found me, writhing around and frothing at the mouth, and this hero used his passcode to override the system and activate an emergency unplug. However, the sudden abortion sparked an electrical feedback that travelled through my wrugs and straight to my heart, stopping it. The guy pulled me free of the chair and administered CPR. He gave my chest a beating in the process of restarting my heart and this explained why, when I woke up, my chest felt like it had been caved in by an enormous weight.

I had a sternal fracture and four cracked ribs as well as myocardial and pulmonary contusions. My doctor told me that these injuries were similar to what someone would suffer in an auto accident. He said it was unlikely a man could have broken my sternum through CPR. He didn't say it like he thought there was something strange going on or anything; he said it more like it was a curious fact. But I have to tell you, (since I'm writing this to be honest) when he told me that I felt like some sort of truth was clicking into place and I was sure – I *am* sure – that what I was told happened and what actually happened are two different things.

I guess it probably seems odd, me saying this now, but I feel kind of shy to write down what I think. You're probably thinking that's nuts after I've written about everything else that happened. Even the parts that make me sick. Those parts keep coming back on me. I can't seem to forget any of it.

Anyway. I was in hospital for over a week. I healed up really well, though, and eventually I was allowed to go back to school. I remember the first day back. I swallowed. I was nervous. They had all been on sims in the word museum but none of them had been hospitalised afterwards. I was expecting extreme hilarity at my expense. So it really surprised me when nobody said anything to me at all. Nothing. Apparently people had tried to keep what had happened to me quiet, but since so many kids go to the word museum at weekends some of them saw me being carried out by the ambulance people. Word spread fast that I'd fallen unconscious in the word museum and that I had to be hospitalised, but no one knew why and no one seemed to think that what happened was related in any way to the word museum or the sims. People prefer not to think things like that.

So everyone knew but no one seemed to find it funny and no one seemed to want to know the details. I was politely ignored by everyone, even Kel, who seemed to have completely disappeared. I think I was most surprised by my teachers. They acted like I hadn't missed any time at all. In fact, they seemed to be wilfully trying not to see me. I puzzled over it a bit. I even asked my parents, but they thought I was imagining things. So that left me pretty much alone with my thoughts and so you can see how I got to writing this all down for you, unknown reader. My thoughts were taken up with one thing only: everything that had happened in sim.

Now, you've read what I saw, and what I experienced. A diluted version of it all. So I reckon you've seen things it took me a whole lot of remembering to work out. You've probably made connections after seeing the same names and the different times, and you've seen the contrasts and the darkness. Maybe you've worked out why, after all of that, I found myself alone, with no one to talk to. But the truth is, I don't care about whatever it is that's wrong here. I'm not telling you all of this so that you can work on a conspiracy theory or something like that.

Look. At the beginning of all of this I became a cat. I told you about the 'aliveness' I experienced then. But that was nothing compared with the depth of feeling, both physically and emotionally, that I experienced of the word 'wild'. And that sounds great, I know it does, but I wouldn't wish it on anyone. And this isn't because I'm selfish. It isn't that I don't want people to enjoy what they want to enjoy. I don't want to stop anyone from having rich moments. I just want people to have their *own* moments. See, I think there were places in my ride that stole from me. There were moments I experienced in sim that I was supposed to have in the real world. Moments that I was going to enjoy, or suffer through, for the first time, as myself. But I've had those moments through other people, now. Through other things, even. And I can't forget them. I feel different now: older, violated, strange, and if I'm perfectly honest, I feel sad that I've lost that clarity of feeling the sim gave me.

I've been back at school for over a month. I stay pretty quiet, keep myself to myself, but I can't help watching all the wild kids. I keep seeing Cliff wandering the hallways like a king, all the other kids flanking him. They joke and laugh and love. They live. At the weekends I often hang out outside the word museum. That might seem weird to you but I'm still trying to work things out. I watch the wild ones and the wannabes rush into the place as soon as they can get there. They usually stay until closing time. I don't know what they're seeing, what they're tasting, smelling, feeling. I have no idea what they're gaining or losing, but I feel frightened for them.

I think about them all and I sit on the steps up on that hill and look out at this little town. Man made. 'Natural'. I can't see beyond the town walls, but I imagine what the whole world looks like sometimes: bubbles of life, safely enclosed, and pure wilderness thriving around us, unseen, unheard, unknown. We're hiding from it all. It frightens us. But we're perfectly happy to plug into machines and let something we don't understand take us over for a bit. Shit. You know, I swear a lot these days. That's kind of funny... Look, I don't know what I'm trying to say to you. I don't know what I want you to take from this. All I know is that this transmission has made me feel less alone for a time. And now it's over. Time to get back to the real world.

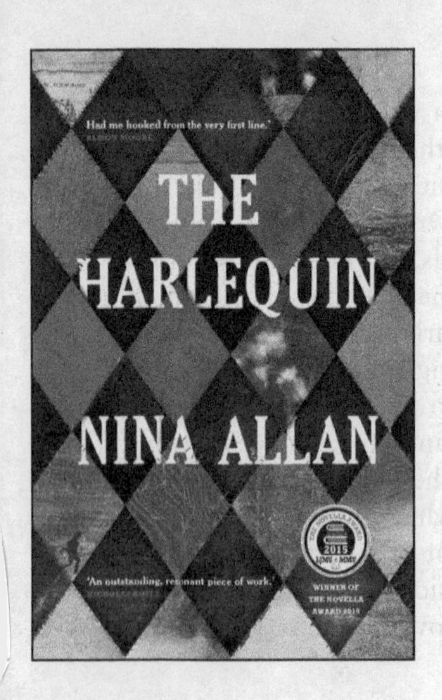

WINNER The Novella Award 2015

'Beaumont felt chilled suddenly, in spite of the fire... Most likely it was the thing's mouth, red-lipped and fiendishly grinning...'

'Had me hooked from the very first line.' **Alison Moore**

'An outstanding, resonant piece of work.' **Nicholas Royle**

ISBN: 9781910124383
RRP: £7.99
Also available in eBook

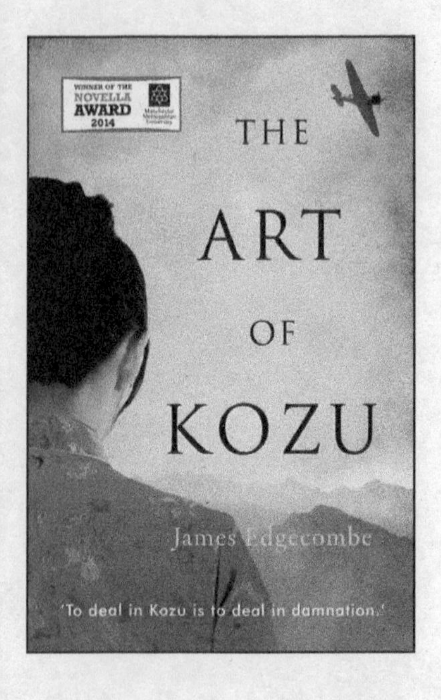

WINNER The Novella Award 2014

With the war over, interest is renewed in the art of Yuichiro Kozu. Can the truth really be understood from a painting, or is a story also required . . . ?

'Steeped in the culture of Japan and written in an elegant style.'
World Literature Today

ISBN: 9781910124000
RRP: £6.99
Also available in eBook